KU-305-355

A GROOM WORTH WAITING FOR

BY

SOPHIE PEMBROKE

WARWICKSHIRE
COUNTY LIBRARY

CONTROL No.

MILLS & BOON

All rights reserved including the right of reproduction in whole or in part in any form. This edition is published by arrangement with Harlequin Books S.A.

This is a work of fiction. Names, characters, places, locations and incidents are purely fictional and bear no relationship to any real life individuals, living or dead, or to any actual places, business establishments, locations, events or incidents. Any resemblance is entirely coincidental.

This book is sold subject to the condition that it shall not, by way of trade or otherwise, be lent, resold, hired out or otherwise circulated without the prior consent of the publisher in any form of binding or cover other than that in which it is published and without a similar condition including this condition being imposed on the subsequent purchaser.

® and TM are trademarks owned and used by the trademark owner and/or its licensee. Trademarks marked with ® are registered with the United Kingdom Patent Office and/or the Office for Harmonisation in the Internal Market and in other countries.

First published in Great Britain 2014
by Mills & Boon, an imprint of Harlequin (UK) Limited,
Large Print edition 2014
Eton House, 18-24 Paradise Road,
Richmond, Surrey, TW9 1SR

© 2014 Sophie Pembroke

ISBN: 978-0-263-24134-1

Harlequin (UK) Limited's policy is to use papers that are natural, renewable and recyclable products and made from wood grown in sustainable forests. The logging and manufacturing processes conform to the legal environmental regulations of the country of origin.

Printed and bound in Great Britain
by CPI Antony Rowe, Chippenham, Wiltshire

For Emma, Helen & Mary.

CHAPTER ONE

'WHAT DO YOU MEAN, he's coming here?' Thea Morrison clasped her arms around her body, as if the action could somehow hide the fact that she was wearing a ridiculously expensive, pearl-encrusted, embroidered ivory wedding dress, complete with six-foot train. 'He can't!'

Her sister rolled her big blue eyes. 'Oh, calm down. He just told me to tell you that you're late to meet with the wedding planner and if you aren't there in five minutes he'll come and get you,' Helena said.

'Well, stop him!'

No, that wouldn't work. Nothing stopped Flynn Ashton when he really wanted something. He was always polite, but utterly tenacious. That was why his father had appointed him his right-hand man at Morrison-Ashton media. And why she was marrying him in the first place.

'Get me out of this dress before he gets here!'

'I don't know why you care so much,' Helena said, fumbling with the zip at the back of the dress. 'It's not like this is a real wedding anyway.'

'In two days there'll be a priest, a cake, some flowers, and a legally binding pre-nup saying otherwise.' Thea wriggled to try and get the strapless dress down over her hips. 'And everyone knows it's bad luck for the groom to see the bride in the wedding dress before the big day.'

It was more than a superstition, it was a rule. Standard Operating Procedure for weddings. Flynn was not seeing this dress a single moment before she walked down the aisle of the tiny Tuscan church at the bottom of the hill from the villa. Not one second.

'Which is why he sent me instead.'

Thea froze, her blood suddenly solid in her veins. She knew that voice. It might have been eight years since she'd heard it, but she hadn't forgotten. Any of it.

The owner of that voice really shouldn't be seeing her in nothing but her wedding lingerie. Especially since she was marrying his brother in two days.

Yanking the dress back up over her ivory corset, Thea held it tight against her chest and stared at him. 'I thought you weren't coming.' But there he was. Large as life and twice as... Hell, she couldn't even lie in her brain and finish that with *ugly*. He looked...grown up. Not twenty-one and angry at everything any more. More relaxed, more in control.

And every inch as gorgeous as he'd always been. Curse him.

Helena laughed. 'Eight years and that's all you have to say to him?' Skipping across the room, blonde hair bouncing, she wrapped her arms around him and pressed a kiss against his cheek. 'It's good to see you, Zeke.'

'Little Helena, all grown up.' Zeke returned the hug, but his gaze never left Thea's. 'It's good to see you too. And rather more of your sister than I'd bargained on.'

There was a mocking edge in his voice. As if she'd planned for him to walk in on her in her underwear. He wasn't even supposed to be in the country! Flynn had told her he wouldn't come and she'd been flooded with relief—even if she could never explain why to her husband-to-be. But now here Zeke was, staring at her, and Thea had never felt so exposed.

She clutched the dress tighter—a barrier between them. 'Well, I was expecting your brother.'

'Your fiancé,' Zeke said. 'Of course. Sorry. Seems he thought I should get started with my best man duties a few days early.'

Thea blinked. '*You're* Flynn's best man?'

'Who else would he choose?' He said it as if he hadn't been gone for eight years. As if he'd never taunted Flynn about not being a real Ashton, only an adopted one, a fall-back plan. As if he hadn't sworn that he was never coming back.

'Anyone in the world.' Quite literally. Flynn could have appointed the Russian Prime Minister as his best man and Thea would have been less surprised.

'He chose his brother,' Helena said, giving Thea her usual *are you crazy?* look. She'd perfected it at fifteen and had been employing it with alarming regularity ever since. 'What's so weird about that?'

Helena hadn't been there. She'd been—what? Sixteen? Too young or too self-absorbed to get involved in the situation, or to realise what was going on. Thea had wanted to keep it from her—from everybody—even then. Of course with hindsight even at sixteen Helena had probably had a better idea about men than Thea had at eighteen. Or now, at twenty-six. But Helena had been dealing with her own issues then.

'So, you're here for the wedding?' Thea said.

Zeke raised his eyebrows. 'What else could I possibly be here for?'

She knew what he wanted her to say, or at least to think. That he'd come back for her. To tell her she'd made the wrong decision eight years ago and she was making a worse one now. To stop her making the biggest mistake of her life.

Except Thea knew full well she'd already made that. And it had nothing to do with Zeke Ashton.

No, she had her suspicions about Zeke's return, but she didn't think he was there for her. If he'd come back to the family fold there had to be something much bigger at stake than a teenage rebellion of a relationship that had been dead for almost a decade.

'I need to get changed.'

Keeping the dress clasped tight to her body, Thea stepped off the platform and slipped behind the screen to change back into her sundress from earlier. She could hear Helena and Zeke chatting lightly outside, making out his amused tone more than the words he spoke. That was one thing that hadn't changed. The world was still a joke to him—her family most of all.

Hanging the beautiful wedding dress up carefully on its padded hanger, Thea stepped back and stared at it. Her fairytale dress, all sparkle and shine. The moment she put it on she became a different person. A wife, perhaps. That dress, whatever it had cost, was worth every penny if it made her into that person, made her *fit*.

This time, this dress, this wedding…it had to be the one that stuck. That bought her the place in the world she needed. Nothing else she'd tried had worked.

Shaking her head, Thea tugged the straps of her sundress up over her shoulders, thankful for a moment or two to regroup. To remind herself that this didn't change anything. So Zeke was there, lurking around their Tuscan villa. So what? He wasn't there for *her*. She was still marrying Flynn. She belonged with Flynn. She had the dress; she had the plan. She had Helena at her side to make sure she said, wore and did the right thing at the right time. This was it. This villa, this wedding. This was where she was supposed to be. Everything was in its right place—apart from Zeke Ashton.

Well, he could just stay out of her perfect picture, thank you very much. Besides, the villa was big enough she probably wouldn't even notice he was in residence most of the time. Not a problem.

Sandals on, Thea smoothed down her hair and stepped back out. 'Now, if you'll excuse me, I have a meeting with the wedding planner to attend.'

'Of course,' Zeke said, with that infuriating mocking smile still in place. 'We wouldn't dream of delaying the blushing bride.'

Thea nodded sharply. She was *not* blushing.

She'd made a promise to herself eight years ago. A decision. And part of that decision meant that Zeke Ashton would never be able to make her blush again.

That part of her life was dead and buried.

Just two days until the wedding. Two more days—that was all. Two days until Thea Morrison got her happily-ever-after.

'In fact,' Zeke said, 'why don't I walk you there? We can catch up.'

Thea's jaw clenched. 'That would be lovely,' she lied.

Two days and this miserable week would be over. Thea couldn't wait.

She barely looked like Thea. With her dark hair straightened and pinned back, her slender arms and legs bronzed to the perfect shade of tan… she looked like someone else. Zeke studied her as she walked ahead of him, long strides clearly designed to get her away from his company as soon as physically possible.

Did she even remember the time when that had been the last thing she'd wanted? When she'd smile and perform her hostess duties at her father's dinner parties and company barbecues, then sneak off to hide out somewhere private, often dark and cosy, with him…? Whoever she'd pretended to be for their parents—the good girl, the dutiful daughter—when they were alone Zeke had seen the real Thea. Seen glimpses of the woman he'd always believed she'd become.

Zeke shook his head. Apparently he'd been

wrong. Those times were gone. And as he watched Thea—all high-heeled sandals, sundress and God only knew what underneath, rather than jeans, sneakers and hot pink knickers—he knew the girl he'd loved was gone, too. The Thea he'd fallen in love with would never have agreed to marry his brother, whatever their respective fathers' arguments for why it was a good idea. She'd wanted love—true love. And for a few brief months he'd thought she'd found it.

He'd been wrong again, though.

Lengthening his own stride, he caught up to her easily. She might have long legs, but his were longer. 'So,' he asked casually, 'how many people are coming to this shindig, anyway?'

'Shindig?' Thea stopped walking. 'Did you just call my wedding a *shindig*?'

Zeke shrugged. Nice to know he could still get under her skin so easily. It might make the next couple of days a little more fun. Something had to. 'Sorry. I meant to say your fairytale-worthy perfect day, when thou shalt join your body in heavenly communion with the deepest love of your heart and soul. How many people are coming to *that*?'

Colour rose in her cheeks, filling him with a strange sense of satisfaction. It was childish, maybe. But he wasn't going to let her get away with pretending that this was a real, true love-match. It was business, just like everything else the Morrisons and the Ashtons held dear.

Including him, these days. Even if his business wasn't the family one any more.

'Two hundred and sixty-eight,' Thea said, her tone crisp. 'At the last count.'

'Small and intimate, then?' Zeke said. 'Just how my father likes things. Where are you putting them all up? I mean, I get that this place is enormous, but still…I can't imagine *your* guests doubling up on camp beds on the veranda.'

'We've booked out the hotel down the road. There'll be executive coaches and cabs running back and forth on the day.'

A small line had formed between her eyebrows, highlighting her irritation. That was new, too.

'Why do you care, anyway?'

'I'm the best man,' he reminded her. 'It's my job to know these things.'

That, apparently, was the line that did it. Spinning round to face him straight on, Thea planted her hands on her hips and scowled at him. 'Why are you here, Zeke? And don't give me some line about brotherly duties. I know full well what you think about Flynn.'

Did she? Maybe she could enlighten *him*, then. Zeke had long since given up trying to make sense of his relationship with his adopted brother. After he'd left home he'd spent months lying awake thinking about it. Wondering if he could have changed things if he'd realised sooner, before that last conversation with his father that had driven him away for good... But in the end the past was the past. He'd had to move on. Besides, this wasn't about him and Flynn. It was about Flynn and Thea.

'Well, if you're not going to buy brotherly affection, I doubt you'll go for family loyalty either.' He shrugged. 'I'm far more interested in what our fathers said to get you to agree to marry the Great Pretender.'

'Don't call him that,' Thea snapped. 'It wasn't funny when we were kids, and it's not funny now. And is it so hard to believe that I might actually *want* to marry Flynn?'

'Yes,' Zeke said automatically. And not just because she wasn't marrying *him*, whatever his business partner, Deb, said.

'Well, I do.' Thea stared at him mulishly, as if she were barely resisting the urge to add, *So there!*

Zeke leant back against the sunny yellow stone of the hallway, staring down through the arches towards the terrace beyond and the green vines snaking up the trellis. Clearly they were no longer in a hurry to get to the meeting, which gave him a chance to find out what had been going on around here lately.

'Really?' he said, folding his arms across his chest. 'So you're saying that the fact that your marriage will merge both sides of the business for all time, and give your heirs total control, hasn't even crossed your mind?'

Thea pulled a face. 'Of course it has.'

'And if it hadn't I'm sure your father would have made it very clear.' Thomas Morrison was always very good about making his daughter understand the implications of her actions, as Zeke remembered it. Especially when they could benefit him—or threatened to inconvenience him.

'But that doesn't mean it wasn't my decision,' Thea said.

And suddenly all Zeke could think about was the last decision Thea had made, right before he'd skipped out on the family, the business and the rest of his life.

'Of course not,' he said, with a sharp, bitter taste in his mouth at the words. 'I know you like to weigh your decisions very carefully. Make sure you're choosing the most beneficial option.'

Thea's jaw dropped slightly. What? Had she expected him not to notice exactly how mercenary her behaviour was? Maybe eight years ago she might have fooled him, but he knew better now. He knew exactly what mattered to her—and it wasn't him.

'What, exactly, are you trying to say?' She bit the words out, as if she were barely holding back a tirade of insulted pride. 'And I'd think very carefully before answering.'

Zeke gave her his most blinding smile. 'Exactly what you think I'm trying to say. That suddenly it makes an awful lot of sense why you chose to stay here instead of coming away with me eight years ago. What was the point once you knew I wasn't the heir any more?' He shrugged, nonchalantly, knowing it would irritate her even more. 'Gotta say, though…I'm surprised it took you this long to bag Flynn.'

She was going to explode. Literally just pop with rage and frustration, spilling bitterness and anger all over the expensively rustic scrubbed walls of this beautiful villa.

Except that would probably make Zeke Ashton smirk even more. So, instead, Thea took a deep breath and prepared to lie.

'As hard as it may be for you to believe, I am in love with your brother.' Her voice came out calm and cool, and Thea felt a small bubble of pride swelling up amongst all the fury. There'd been a time when any words Zeke had spoken to her had provoked an extreme reaction. When they were kids it had usually been annoyance, or anger. Then, when they were teenagers, that annoyance had suddenly become attraction, and then anger, arousal… By the time he'd left…all sorts of other complicated reactions had come into play.

But not any more. Now she was an adult, in control of her own life and making her own decisions. Zeke Ashton's barbs and comments had no power over her any longer. It felt incredibly freeing.

'Love?' Zeke raised an eyebrow. 'You know, I'm starting to think you've got your definition of that word wrong.'

'Trust me, I know *exactly* what it means.' Love meant the incredible pain of loss when it was gone. Or the uncertainty of never knowing if it was returned. It baffled Thea why so many people thought love was a good thing.

'Really? Well, I'm sure I'm just thrilled that you've finally found true love. Guess I was just a practice run.'

Thea's stomach rolled at the reminder. It wasn't that she'd thought he'd forgotten their teenage fling, or even forgiven her for the way it had ended—he'd made it very clear in the half-hour he'd been in the villa that neither had happened. But she hadn't expected him to want to actually *talk* about it. Weren't men supposed to be strong and silent on matters of the heart? Suffering in silence, and all that?

Except Zeke had always loved the sound of his

own voice. Apparently that hadn't changed, even if nearly everything else had.

'That was a long time ago, Zeke. We were kids.' Too far in the past to bring up now, surely? Even for Zeke, with his ridiculous need to *talk* about everything. 'We've both moved on. We're different people now.'

'Want to throw in a few more clichés with that?' Zeke shook his head. 'Look, you can rewrite history any way you like. And, trust me, I'm not here to try and win you back—even to get one over on Flynn. But you're not going to convince me that this is anything but a business deal with rings.'

'You're wrong,' Thea lied. 'And you'll see that. But…'

'But?' Zeke asked, one eyebrow raised again in that mocking expression that drove her crazy. 'But what?'

'Even if it was a business deal…what would be wrong with that? As long as we both know what we're getting into…' She shrugged. 'There are worse reasons to get married.'

'Maybe.' Zeke gave her a slow smile—the one that used to make her insides melt. 'But there are so many better reasons, too.'

* * *

'Like love,' Thea said, apparently still determined to stick to her story.

Zeke didn't buy it, and knew he wouldn't, no matter how hard she tried to convince him. He knew what Thea in love looked like, and this wasn't it.

At least not his Thea. The old Thea. He shook his head. He couldn't let doubt in now. The only thing in his life that had never let him down was gut instinct. He had to trust himself, especially since he couldn't trust anyone else. Not even Thea.

'Love's the big one,' Zeke agreed. 'But it's not the only thing that counts. Trust. Respect. Common values—'

'We have those too,' Thea broke in.

'Sexual compatibility,' Zeke finished, smirking when her mouth snapped shut. 'That's always important for long-term happiness, I find.'

Her gaze hardened. 'Really? And how's that working out for you? I can't help but notice you've come to my wedding alone, after all.'

He had a comeback for that somewhere, he was sure. But since Flynn arrived at that moment—

cool, collected, and always an inch and a half taller than Zeke—he didn't have to search for it.

'Zeke! You made it.' Flynn stepped up and held out a hand, but before Zeke could even take it Thea had latched on to her fiancé's other arm, smiling up at him in a sickeningly adoring manner.

Keeping the handshake as perfunctory as possible, Zeke moved out of their circle of love and into his own space of scepticism. 'How could I resist the opportunity to be the best man for once? Might be the only chance I get.'

Flynn's smile stiffened a little at that, but he soldiered on regardless. Always so keen to play up the family loyalty—to be a part of the family he'd never really thought he belonged in. Zeke would have thought that their father choosing Flynn over him would have gone a long way to convincing his brother that there was only one golden boy in the family, and that blood didn't matter at all.

'I wouldn't want anyone but my brother beside me on such an important day,' Flynn said.

He didn't even sound as if he was lying, which Zeke thought was quite an accomplishment.

'Really? Because I have to admit I was kind of

surprised to be asked.' Zeke glanced at Thea, who gave him an *I knew it!* look. 'Not as surprised as Thea was to see me here, of course,' he added, just because he could. She glared at him, and snuggled closer against Flynn's arm. There was absolutely no chemistry between them at all. And not a chance in hell they'd ever slept together. What on earth was Thea doing with him?

'You said he wasn't coming,' Thea pointed out—rather accusingly, Zeke thought.

'I wasn't sure he would,' Flynn admitted, glancing down at Thea with an apologetic smile.

Zeke wasn't sure he liked the idea of them talking about him in his absence. What had she said? How much had she told him?

'But, Zeke, you were the one who left us, remember? Not the other way round. Of course I asked you. You're my brother.'

'And that's the only reason?' Zeke asked. An uncomfortable feeling wriggled in his chest at the reminder of his disappearance, but he pushed it aside. He hadn't had a choice. His father had made his position very clear, and that position had taken any other options Zeke might have had off the table. He'd only hung around long enough to waste his time talking to Thea that same night, then he'd been gone. And nobody looking at Zeke now, at how far he'd come and how much he'd achieved, could say that he'd made a mistake by leaving.

Flynn didn't answer his question. With a sigh, he said, 'Dad's got a dinner planned for tonight, by the way. To welcome you home.'

Zeke appreciated the warning too much to point out that a luxury Tuscan villa belonging to some client or another wasn't actually 'home', no matter how many swimming pools it had. 'A prodigal son type thing? Hope he's found a suitably fatted calf.'

'I'm sure there was some poor animal just *begging* to be sacrificed on your behalf,' Thea said. 'But before then don't we have a meeting with the wedding planner to get to, darling?'

The endearment sounded unnatural on her tongue, and Flynn actually looked uncomfortable as she said it. Nobody would ever believe these two actually loved each other or wanted to see each other naked. Watching them, Zeke couldn't even see that they'd ever met before, let alone been childhood friends. He could imagine them on their wedding night—all unnatural politeness and a wall of pillows down the middle of the bed. If it wasn't Thea doing the marrying, it would be hilarious.

'She had to leave,' Flynn said. 'But I think we sorted out all the last-minute details. I said you'd call her later if there was anything you were concerned about.'

'I'm sure it's all fine,' Thea said, smiling serenely.

Even that seemed false. Shouldn't a woman getting married in two days be a little bit more involved in the details?

A door opened somewhere, slamming shut again as Hurricane Helena came blowing through.

'Are you guys still here?' she asked, waves of blonde hair bobbing past her shoulders. 'Shouldn't you all be getting ready for dinner? Thea, I had the maid press your dress for tonight. It's hanging in your room. Can I borrow your bronze shoes, though?'

'Of course,' Thea said, just as she always had to Helena, ever since their mother had died.

Zeke wondered if she even realised she did it.

'Come on, I'll find them for you now.'

As the women made their way down the corridor Helena spun round, walking backwards for a moment. 'Hope you brought your dinner jacket, Zeke. Apparently this welcome home bash is a formal affair.'

So his father had been sure he'd come, even if no one else had. Why else would he have set up a formal dinner for his arrival?

Helena turned back, slipping a hand through her sister's arm and giggling. Thea, Zeke couldn't help but notice, didn't look back at all.

Beside him, Flynn gave him an awkward smile. He'd always hated having to wear a bow tie, Zeke remembered suddenly. At least someone else would be miserable that evening.

'I'll see you at dinner,' Flynn said, setting off down another corridor.

'Can't wait.' Zeke's words echoed in the empty hallway. 'Gonna be a blast.'

CHAPTER TWO

THEA SHOULD HAVE known this wasn't just about shoes.

'So…Zeke coming home. Bit of a shock, huh?' Helena said, lounging back on Thea's ridiculously oversized bed.

'Yep.' Thea stuck her head in the closet and tried to find her bronze heels. Had she even packed them?

'Even though old Ezekiel Senior has planned a welcome home dinner?'

'I told you—Flynn didn't think he'd come,' Thea explained. 'So neither did I.'

'So Flynn was just as shocked?' Helena asked, too innocently.

'Probably,' Thea said. 'He just hides it better.'

'He hides *everything* better,' Helena muttered. 'But, to be honest, he didn't seem all that surprised when I told him Zeke had arrived.'

Thea bashed her head on the wardrobe door.

Rubbing her hand over the bump, she backed out into the room again. 'Then maybe he just had more faith that his brother would do the right thing than I did. I really don't think I brought those bronze shoes.'

'No? What a shame. I'll just have to wear my pewter ones.' Helena sat up, folding her legs under her. 'Why don't you trust Zeke? I thought you two were pretty close before he left.'

Thea stared at her sister. She'd known all along she didn't have the stupid shoes, hadn't she? She'd just wanted an excuse to quiz her about Zeke. Typical.

'We were friends,' she allowed. 'We all were. Hard not to be when they were over at our house all the time.'

'Or we were there,' Helena agreed. 'Especially after Mum…'

'Yeah.'

Isabella Ashton had quickly taken pity on the poor, motherless Morrison girls. She'd been more than happy to educate fourteen-year-old Thea in the correct way to run her father's household and play the perfect hostess. At least until Thea had proved she wasn't up to the task and Isabella had taken over all together. Thea would have been relived, if she hadn't had to bear the brunt of her father's disappointment ever since.

And been made to feel like an outsider in my own home.

Thea swallowed and batted the thought away. Helena probably didn't remember that part of it. As far as she was concerned Isabella had just made sure they were supplied with any motherly advice they needed. Whether they wanted it or not.

Thea moved over to the dressing table, looking for the necklace Isabella had given her for her eighteenth birthday. The night Zeke had left. She'd wear it tonight, along with her own mother's ring. Isabella always appreciated gestures like that.

'And you've really not spoken to Zeke at all since he left?' Helena asked.

Thea wondered how much her sister suspected about her relationship with Flynn's brother. Too much, it seemed.

'Not once,' she said firmly, picking up Isabella's necklace. 'Not once in eight years.'

'Strange.' Helena slipped off the bed and came up behind her, taking the ends of the chain from her to fasten it behind her neck. 'Do you think that's why he's come back now? Because you're getting married?'

'Well, he was invited, so I'm thinking that was probably the reason.'

'No,' Helena said, and something about her sister's quiet, firm voice made Thea look up and meet her eyes in the mirror. 'I meant because *you're* getting married.'

Thea swallowed. 'He didn't come and visit the last time I almost got married.'

'Or the time before that,' Helena said, cheerfully confirming her view of Thea as a serial fiancée. 'But then, those times you weren't marrying his brother.' The words *And you didn't go through with it...* went unsaid.

Thea dropped down onto the dressing table stool. Wouldn't that be just like Zeke—not to care that she might marry someone else as long as it wasn't a personal slight to him? But did he even know about the others? If he did, she predicted she'd be subjected to any number of comments and jibes on the subject. *Perfect.* Because she hadn't had enough of that at work, or from her friends, or even in the gossip pages.

Only Helena had never said anything about it. Her father had just torn up the pre-nups, asked his secretary to cancel the arrangements, and said, 'Next time, perhaps?' After the last one even Thea had had to admit to herself that she was better off sticking to business than romance.

It was just that each time she'd thought she'd found a place she could belong. Someone to belong to. Until it had turned out that she wasn't what they really wanted after all. She was never quite right—never quite good enough in the end.

Except for Flynn. Flynn knew exactly what he was getting, and why. He'd chosen it, debated it, drawn up a contract detailing exactly what the deal entailed. And that was exactly what Thea needed. No confused expectations, no unspoken agreements—this was love done business-style. It suited her perfectly.

Zeke would think it was ridiculous if he knew. But she was pretty sure that Zeke had a better reason for returning than just mocking her love life.

'That's not why he's back.'

'Are you sure?' Helena asked. 'Maybe this is just the first time he thought you might actually go through with it.'

'You make me sound like a complete flake.' Which was fair, probably. Except she'd always been so sure…until it had become clear that the men she was supposed to marry weren't.

Helena sighed and picked up a hairbrush from the dressing table, running it through her soft golden waves. Thea had given up wishing she had hair like that years ago. Boring brown worked fine for her.

'Not a flake,' Helena said, teasing out a slight tangle. 'Just…uncertain.'

'"Decisionally challenged", Dad says.'

Helena laughed. 'That's not true. You had a perfectly good reason not to marry those guys.'

'Because it turned out one was an idiot who wanted my money and the other was cheating on me?' And she hadn't seen it, either time, until it had been almost too late. Hadn't realised until it had been right in front of her that she couldn't be enough of a lover or a woman for one of them, or human enough to be worth more than hard cash to the other. Never valuable enough in her own right just to be loved.

'Because you didn't love them.' Helena put

down the brush. 'Which makes me wonder again why exactly you're marrying Flynn.'

Thea looked away from the mirror. 'We'll be good together. He's steady, sensible, gentle. He'll make a great husband and father. Our families will finally be one, just like everyone always wanted them to be. It's good for the business, good for our parents, and good for us. This time I know exactly what I'm signing up for. That's how I know that I've made the right decision.'

This time. This one time. After a lifetime of bad ones, Thea knew that this decision had to stick. This was the one that would give her a proper family again, and a place within it. Flynn needed her—needed the legitimacy she gave him. Thea was well aware of the irony: he needed her Morrison bloodline to cement his chances of inheriting the company, while she needed him, the adopted Ashton son, to earn back her place in her own family.

It was messed up, yes. But at least they'd get to be messed up together.

Helena didn't say anything for a long moment. Was she thinking about all the other times Thea had got it wrong? Not just with men, but with everything…with Helena. That one bad decision that Helena still had to live with the memory of every day?

But when she glanced back at her sister's reflection Helena gave her a bright smile and said, 'You'd better get downstairs for cocktails. And I'd better go and find my pewter shoes. I'll meet you down there, okay?'

Thea nodded, and Helena paused in the doorway.

'Thea? Maybe he just wanted to see you again. Get some closure—that sort of thing.'

As the door swung shut behind her sister Thea wished she was right. That Zeke was ready to move on, at last, from all the slights and the bitterness that had driven him away and kept him gone for so long. Maybe things would never be as they were when they were kids, but perhaps they could find a new family dynamic—one that suited them all.

And it all started with her wedding.

Taking a deep breath, Thea headed down to face her family, old and new, and welcome the prodigal son home again. Whether he liked it or not.

* * *

It was far too hot to be wearing a dinner jacket. Whose stupid idea was this, anyway? Oh, that was right. His father's.

Figured.

Zeke made his way down the stairs towards the front lounge and, hopefully, alcohol, torn between the impulse to rush and get it over with, or hold back and put it off for as long as possible. What exactly was his father hoping to prove by this dinner?

Zeke couldn't shake the feeling that Flynn's sudden burst of brotherly love might not be the only reason he'd been invited back to the fold for the occasion. Perhaps he'd better stick to just the one cocktail. If his father had an ulterior motive for wanting him there, Zeke needed to be sober when he found out what it was. Then he could merrily thwart whatever plan his dad had cooked up, stand up beside Flynn at this ridiculously fake wedding, and head off into the sunset again. Easy.

He hadn't rushed, but Zeke was still only the second person to make it to the cocktail cabinet. The first, perhaps unsurprisingly, was Thomas Morrison. The old man had always liked a martini before dinner, but as his gaze rose to study Zeke his mouth tightened and Zeke got the odd impression that Thea's dad had been waiting for him.

'Zeke.' Thomas held out a filled cocktail glass. 'So you made it, then.'

Wary, Zeke took the drink. 'You sound disappointed by that, sir.'

'I can't be the only person surprised to see you back.'

Zeke thought of Thea, standing in nothing but the underwear she'd bought for his brother, staring at him as if he'd returned from the dead. Was that really how she thought of him? In the back of his mind he supposed he'd always thought he *would* come back. When he was ready. When he'd proved himself. When he was *enough.* The wedding had just forced his hand a bit.

'I like to think I'm a pleasant surprise,' Zeke said.

Thomas sipped his martini and Zeke felt obliged to follow suit. He wished he hadn't; Thomas clearly liked his drinks a certain way—paint-stripper-strong. He put the glass down on the cocktail bar.

'Well, I think that depends,' Thomas said. 'On

whether you plan to break your mother's heart again.'

Zeke blinked. 'She didn't seem that heartbroken to me.' In fact when she'd greeted him on his arrival she'd seemed positively unflustered. As if he was just one more guest she had to play the perfect hostess to.

'You never did know your mother.' Thomas shook his head.

'But *you* did.' It wasn't a new thought. The two families had always been a touch too close, lived a little too much in each other's pockets. And after his wife's death...well, it hadn't been just Thomas's daughters that Zeke's mother had seemed to want to look after.

'We're old friends, boy. Just like your father and I.'

Was that all? If it was a lie, it was one they'd all been telling themselves for so long now it almost seemed true.

'And I was there for both of them when you abandoned them. I don't think any of us want to go through that again.'

Maybe eight years had warped the old man's memory. No way had his father been in the least bit bothered by his disappearing act—hell, it was probably what he'd wanted. Why else would he have picked Flynn over him to take on the role of his right-hand man at Morrison-Ashton? Except Zeke knew why—even if he didn't understand it. He had heard his father's twisted reasoning from the man's own lips. That was why he'd left.

But he couldn't help but wonder if Zeke leaving hadn't been Ezekiel Senior's plan all along. If he'd *wanted* him to go out in the world and make something of himself. If so, that was exactly what Zeke had done.

But not for his father. For himself.

'So, you think I should stick around this time?' Zeke asked, even though he had no intention of doing so. Once he knew what his father was up to he'd be gone again. Back to his own life and his own achievements. Once he'd proved his point.

'I think that if you plan to leave again you don't want to get too close while you're here.'

The old man's steely gaze locked on to Zeke's, and suddenly Zeke knew this wasn't about his father, or even his mother.

This was about Thea.

Right on cue they heard footsteps on the stairs,

and Zeke turned to see Thea in the doorway, beautiful in a peacock-blue gown that left her shoulders bare, with her dark hair pinned back from her face and her bright eyes sharp.

Thomas clapped him on the shoulder and said, 'Welcome home, Zeke.' But the look he shot at Thea left Zeke in no doubt of the words he left unsaid. *Just don't stay too long.*

The air in the lounge felt too heavy, too tightly pressed around the stilted conversation between the three of them—until Helena breezed in wearing the beautiful pewter shoes that had been a perfect match for her dress all along. She fixed drinks, chatting and smiling all the way, and as she pressed another martini into their father's hand some of the tension seemed to drop and Thea found she could breathe properly again.

At least until she let her eyes settle on Zeke. Maybe that was the problem. If she could just keep her eyes closed and not see the boy she remembered loving, or the man he'd turned into, she'd be just fine. But the way he stood there, utterly relaxed and unconcerned, his suit outlining a body that had grown up along with the boy, she wanted to know him. Wanted to explore the differences. To find out exactly who he was now, just for this moment in time, before he left again.

Stop it. Engaged to his brother, remember?

Flynn arrived moments later, his mother clutching his arm, and suddenly things felt almost easy. Flynn and Helena both had that way about them; they could step into a room and make it better. They knew how to settle people, how to make them relax and smile even when there were a million things to be fretting about.

Flynn had always been that way, Thea remembered. Always the calm centre of the family, offset by Zeke's spinning wild brilliance—and frustration. For Helena it had come later.

Through their whole childhood Thea had been the responsible eldest child, the sensible one, at least when people were looking. And all the while Helena had thrown tantrums and caused chaos. Until Thea had messed up and resigned her role. Somehow Helena had seemed to grow to fill it, even as Isabella had taken over the job of mother, wife and hostess that Thea had been deemed unsuitable for. If it hadn't been for her role at the company, Thea wondered sometimes if they'd have bothered keeping her around at all. They certainly hadn't seemed to need her. At least not until Flynn needed a bride with an appropriate bloodline.

'Are we ready to go through for dinner?' Isabella asked the room at large. 'My husband will be joining us shortly. He just has a little business to finish up.'

What business was more important than this? Hadn't Ezekiel insisted on this huge welcome home feast for his prodigal son? The least he could do was show up and be part of it. Thea wanted nothing more than for Zeke to disappear back to wherever he'd been for eight years, and *she* was still there.

Thea glanced up at Zeke and found him already watching her, eyebrows raised and expression amused. He slid in alongside her as they walked through to dinner.

'Offended on my behalf by my father's tardiness?' he asked. 'It's sweet, but quite unnecessary. The whole evening might be a lot more pleasant if he *doesn't* join us.'

'I wasn't…it just seemed a little rude, that's all.'

'Rude. Of course.'

He offered his arm for her to hold, but Thea ignored it. The last thing she needed was to actually touch Zeke in that suit.

'That's why your face was doing that righteously indignant thing.'

Thea stared at him. '"Righteously indignant thing"?'

'Yeah. Where you frown and your nose wrinkles up and your mouth goes all stern and disapproving.'

'I…I didn't know I did that.'

Zeke laughed, and up ahead Helena turned back to look at them. 'You've always done it,' he said. 'Usually when someone's being mean about me. Or Flynn, or Helena. It's cute. But like I said, in this case unnecessary.'

Thea scowled, then tried to make her face look as neutral as possible. Never mind her traitorous thoughts—apparently now she had to worry about unconscious overprotective facial expressions, too.

There were only six of them for dinner—seven if Ezekiel managed to join them—and they clustered around one end of the monstrously large dining table. Her father took the head, with Isabella at his side and Flynn next to her. Which left Thea sandwiched between Zeke and her father, with Helena on Zeke's other side, opposite Flynn. Thea couldn't help but think place cards might have been a good idea. Maybe she could have set hers in the kitchen, away from everybody...

They'd already made it through the starter before Ezekiel finally arrived. Thea bit her lip as he entered. Would he follow the unspoken boy-girl rule and sit next to Helena? But, no, he moved straight to Flynn's side and, with barely an acknowledgement of Zeke's presence in the room, started talking business with his eldest son.

Thea snuck a glance at Zeke, who continued to play with his soup as if he hadn't noticed his father's entrance.

'Did he already welcome you back?' Thea asked. But she knew Ezekiel Senior had been locked in his temporary office all day, so the chances were slim.

Zeke gave her a lopsided smile. 'You know my father. Work first.'

Why was she surprised? Ezekiel Ashton had always been the same.

'Well, if he's not going to ask you, I will.' Shifting in her seat to face him a little, Thea put on her best interested face. 'So, Zeke… What have you been up to the last eight years?'

'You don't know?' Zeke asked, eyebrows raised. 'Aren't you supposed to be in charge of PR and marketing for the company? I'd have thought it was your business to keep on top of what your competitors are up to.'

Too late Thea realised the trap she'd walked straight into. 'Oh, I know about your *business* life,' she said airily. 'Who doesn't? You set up a company purposely to rival the family business—presumably out of spite. It's the kind of thing the media loves to talk about. But, really, compared to Morrison-Ashton This Minute is hardly considered a serious competitor. More a tiny fish.'

'Beside your shark?' Zeke reached for his wine glass. 'I can see that. But This Minute wasn't ever intended to be a massive media conglomerate. Big companies can't move fast enough for me.'

That made sense. Zeke had never been one for sitting in meetings and waiting for approval on things he wanted to get done. But according to industry gossip even his instant response news website and app This Minute wasn't enough to hold his attention any more.

'I heard you were getting ready to sell.'

'Did you, now?' Zeke turned his attention across the table, to where his father and Flynn were still deep in conversation. 'That explains a lot.'

'Like?'

'Like why my father added his own personal request that I attend to my wedding invitation. He wants to talk about This Minute.'

So *that* was why he was back. Nothing to do with her, or Flynn, or the wedding. Not that she'd really thought it was, but still the knowledge sat heavily in her chest. 'You think he wants to buy it?'

'He's *your* CEO. What do you think?'

It would make sense, Thea had to admit. Their own twenty-four-hour news channels couldn't keep up with the fast response times of internet sites. Buying up This Minute would be cheaper in the long run than developing their own version. And it would bring Zeke back into the family fold...

'Yes, I think he does.'

'Guess we'll find out,' Zeke said. 'If he ever deigns to speak to me.'

'What would you do?' Thea asked as the maid cleared their plates and topped up their wine glasses. 'Would you stay with This Minute?' It was hard to imagine Zeke coming back to work for Morrison-Ashton, even on his own terms. And if he did he'd be there, in her building, every day…

'No.' Zeke's response was firm. 'I'm ready to do something new.' He grinned. 'In fact, I want to do it all over again.'

'Start a new business? Why? Why not just enjoy your success for a while?'

'Like your father?' Zeke nodded at the head of the table, where Thomas was laughing at something Isabella had said.

Thea shook her head. 'My dad was never a businessman—you know that. He provided the money, sat on the board…'

'And left the actual work to my father.' He held up a hand before Thea could object. 'I know, I know. Neither one of them could have done it without the other. Hasn't that always been the legend? They each brought something vital to the table.'

'It worked,' Thea pointed out.

'And now you and Flynn are ready to take it into the next generation. Bring the families together. Spawn the one true heir.'

Thea looked away. 'You need to stop talking about my wedding like this.'

'Why? It's business, isn't it?'

'It's also my future. The rest of my life—and my children's.' That shut him up for a moment, unexpectedly. Thea took advantage of the brief silence to bring the conversation back round to the question he'd so neatly avoided. 'So, you didn't tell me. Why start up another new business?'

Zeke settled back in his chair, the thin stem of his wine glass resting between his fingers. 'I guess it's the challenge. The chance to take something that doesn't even exist yet, build it up and make it fantastic. Make it mine.'

It sounded exciting. Fresh and fun and everything else Zeke seemed to think it would be. But it also sounded to Thea as if Zeke was reaching for something more than just a successful business venture. Something he might never be able to touch, however hard he tried.

'You want to be a success,' she said slowly. 'But,

Zeke, you've already succeeded. And you still want more. How will you know when you've done enough?'

Zeke turned to look at her, his dark eyes more serious than she'd ever seen them. 'I'll know it when I get there.'

But Thea was very afraid that he wouldn't.

CHAPTER THREE

SO NOW HE KNEW. Had Thea told his dad about the rumours, Zeke wondered, or had the old goat had his own spies on the lookout? Either way, his presence in Italy that week suddenly made a lot more sense. Ezekiel Senior wanted This Minute.

And Zeke had absolutely no intention of giving it to him.

As the rest of the guests enjoyed their dessert Zeke left his spoon on the tablecloth and studied his father across the table. How would he couch it? Would he make it sound as if he was doing Zeke a favour? Or would he—heaven forbid—actually admit that Zeke had achieved something pretty great without the backing of Morrison-Ashton? He'd have to wait to find out.

After dinner, Zeke decided. That would be when his father would finally acknowledge the presence of his youngest son. Probably he'd be summoned to the study. But this time he'd get to go on his own terms. For once Ezekiel wanted something he, Zeke, possessed, rather than the other way round.

That, on its own, made it worth travelling to Flynn and Thea's wedding.

Zeke only realised he was smiling when Flynn suddenly looked up and caught his eye. Zeke widened his grin, raising an eyebrow at his brother. So, had dear old dad just broken the news to the golden boy? And did that mean Thea *hadn't* told her beloved about the rumours she'd heard?

Flynn glanced away again, and Zeke reached for his spoon. 'You didn't tell Flynn, then?'

Thea's dropped her spoon against the edge of her bowl with a clatter. 'Tell Flynn what?' she asked, eyes wide.

Interesting. 'Well, I meant about the This Minute sale,' he said. 'But now I'm wondering what else you've been keeping from your fiancé.'

Thea rolled her eyes, but it was too late. He'd already seen her instinctive reaction. She was keeping things from Flynn. Zeke had absolutely no doubt at all.

'I didn't tell Flynn about the sale because it doesn't directly affect him and it's still only a rumour. If your father decides to make a bid for the company I'm sure he'll fill Flynn in at the appropriate time.' Thea looked up at him through her lashes. 'Besides, we don't talk about you.'

'At all?' That hit him somewhere in the middle of his gut and hit hard. Not that he'd been imagining them sitting around the dining table reminiscing about the good old days when Zeke had been there, or anything. But still, despite his initial misgivings over them talking about him in his absence, he thought this might be worse. They didn't talk about him *at all*?

'Apart from Flynn telling me you weren't coming to the wedding? No.' Thea shrugged. 'What would we say? You left.'

And she'd forgotten all about him. Point made. With a sharp jab to the heart.

But of course if they didn't talk about him… 'So you never told Flynn about us, either?'

She didn't look up from her dessert as she answered. 'Why would I? The past is very firmly in the past. And I had no reason to think you would ever come back at all.'

'And now?'

Raising her head, she met his gaze head-on. 'And now there's simply nothing to say.'

'Zeke.'

The voice sounded a little creakier, but no less familiar. Tearing his gaze away from Thea's face, Zeke turned to see his father standing, waiting for him.

'I'd like a word with you in my office, if you would. After eight years…we have a lot to discuss.'

They had one thing to discuss, as far as Zeke was concerned. But he went anyway. How else would he have the pleasure of turning the old man down?

Ezekiel had chosen a large room at the front of the villa for his office—one Zeke imagined was more usually used for drinks and canapés than for business. The oversized desk in the centre had to have been brought in from elsewhere in the house, because it looked utterly out of place.

Zeke considered the obvious visitor's chair, placed across from it, and settled himself into a leather armchair by the empty fireplace instead. He wasn't a naughty child any more, and that meant he didn't have to stare at his father over a forbidding desk, waiting for judgement to be handed down, ever again.

'Sit,' Ezekiel said, long after Zeke had already done so. 'Whisky or brandy?'

'I'd rather get straight down to business,' Zeke said.

'As you wish.' Ezekiel moved towards the drinks cabinet and poured himself a whisky anyway. Zeke resisted the urge to grind his teeth.

Finally, his father came and settled himself into the armchair opposite, placing his glass on the table between them. 'So. You're selling your business.'

'So the rumour mill tells me,' Zeke replied, leaning back in his chair and resting his ankle on his opposite knee.

'I heard more than rumour,' Ezekiel said. 'I heard you were in negotiations with Glasshouse.'

Zeke's shoulders stiffened. Nobody knew that, except Deb and him at the office, the CEO at Glasshouse and his key team. Which meant one or other of them had a leak. Just what he *didn't* need.

'It's true, then.' Ezekiel shook his head. 'Our biggest competitors, Zeke. Why didn't you just come to me directly? Or is this just another way of trying to get my attention?'

Zeke will never stop trying to best his brother. The words, eight years old, still echoed through Zeke's head, however hard he tried to move past them. But he didn't have time for the memory now.

'I haven't needed your attention for the last eight years, Father. I don't need it now.'

'Really?' Ezekiel reached for his whisky glass. 'Are you sure? Because you could have gone any- where, done anything. Yet you stayed in the coun- try and set up a company that directly competed with the family business.'

'I stuck to what I knew,' Zeke countered. Be- cause, okay, annoying his father might have been part of his motivation. But only part.

Ezekiel gave him a long, steady look, and when Zeke didn't flinch said, 'Hmm...'

Zeke waited. *Time to make the offer, old man.*

'I'm sure that you understand that to have my son working with Glasshouse is...unacceptable. But we can fix this. Come work with us. We'll pay whatever Glasshouse is paying and you can run your little company under the Morrison-

Ashton umbrella. In fact, you could lead our whole digital division.'

Somewhere in there, under the 'let me fix your mistakes' vibe, was an actual job offer. A good one. Head of Digital... There was a lot Zeke could do there to bring Morrison-Ashton into the twenty-first century. It would give him enough clout in the company in order not to feel as if Flynn was his boss. And he would be working with Thea every day...

'No, thanks.' Zeke stood up. He didn't need this any more. He'd grown up now. He didn't need his father's approval, or a place at the table, or even to be better than Flynn. He was his own man at last. 'I appreciate the offer, but I'm done with This Minute. Once I sell to Glasshouse I'm on to something new. Something exciting.'

Something completely unconnected to his family. Or Thea's.

'Really?'

Ezekiel looked up at him and Zeke recognised the disappointment in his eyes. It wasn't as if he hadn't seen that peculiar mix of being let down and proved right at the same time before.

'And if I appeal to your sense of family loyalty?'

Zeke barked a laugh. 'Why would you? You never showed *me* any. You gave Flynn all the chances, the job, the trust and the confidence. You wanted me to find my own road.' He crossed to the door, yanking it open. 'Well, Dad, I found it. And it doesn't lead to Morrison-Ashton.'

'Well,' Flynn said, dropping to sit beside her on the cushioned swing seat. 'That was a day.'

'Yes. Yes, it was.' Thea took the mug he offered her and breathed in the heavy smell of the coffee. 'Is this—?'

'Decaf,' Flynn assured her. 'You think I don't know what my wife-to-be likes?'

'Less "likes",' Thea said, taking a cautious sip. Everyone knew that on a normal day she'd be on her third double espresso well before lunch. 'More that I don't need anything else keeping me awake at night right now.'

'Hmm…' Flynn settled against the back of the seat and, careful of her coffee cup, wrapped an arm around Thea's shoulders, pulling her against him. 'Want to tell me what's keeping you awake?'

Thea tucked her legs up underneath her, letting Flynn rock the swing seat forward and back, the motion helping to relax the tension in her body.

They didn't share a room yet; it hadn't really seemed necessary, given the agreement between them. So he didn't have to know exactly how many hours she spent staring at the ceiling every night, just waiting for this wedding to be over, for the papers to be signed and for her future to be set and certain. But on the other hand she was marrying the man. He'd be her companion through life from here on in, and she wanted that companionship badly. Which meant telling him at least part of the truth.

'I guess I'm just nervous about the wedding,' she admitted.

'About marrying me?' Flynn asked. 'Or getting through the day itself?'

'Mostly the latter.' Thea rested her head against his comfortable shoulder and sighed. 'I just want it to be done. For everyone else to leave and for us to enjoy our honeymoon here in peace. You know?'

'I really, really do.'

Thea smiled at the heartfelt tone in his voice. This was why a marriage between them would work far better than any of the other relationships she'd fallen into, been passionate about, then had end horribly. They were a fit—a pair. If they actually loved each other it would be a classically perfect match.

But then, love—passion, emotion, pain—would be what drove them apart, too. No, far better this friendship and understanding. It made for a far more peaceful life.

Or it would. Once they got through the wedding.

'Feeling the strain, huh?' Thea patted Flynn's thigh sympathetically. 'Be grateful. At least my sister didn't walk in on you in your wedding lingerie this morning.'

'I don't have any wedding lingerie,' Flynn pointed out. 'I have the same boring black style I wear every day. Hang on. Did Zeke…?'

'Yep. He said you sent him to fetch me to meet with the wedding planner. So you wouldn't see me in my dress before the big day.'

'Sorry,' Flynn said, even though it obviously wasn't really his fault. 'I just know how important the traditions are to you. I didn't want to upset you.'

Thea waved a hand to brush away his apology, and Flynn reached over to take her empty coffee cup and place it safely on the table beside him.

'It's not your fault. Just something else to make this day difficult.'

'That does explain why he was in such an odd mood this afternoon, though,' Flynn mused. 'All those defensive jokes. He always did have a bit of a crush on you, I think. Even when we were kids.'

A bit of a crush. Thea ducked her head against Flynn's chest to hide her reaction. Had there ever been such an understatement? She'd assumed at first that Flynn had known something of her relationship with his brother—despite their attempts at secrecy it seemed that plenty of others had. But it had quickly become clear he'd no idea. And they'd never talked about him, so she'd been perfectly happy to consign it to the realms of vague memory.

'I don't think that's why,' she said. 'I'm sure it's just being here, seeing everyone again after so long. It must be strange.'

'It was his choice.' Flynn's voice was firm, unforgiving. 'He could have come home at any time.'

'Perhaps.' What had *really* brought Zeke back now? *Was* it his father's summons? Not to satisfy the old man, of course, but to show him how much

Zeke no longer needed him. To deny him whatever it was he wanted just out of spite?

The Zeke she'd seen today hadn't seemed spiteful, though. He was no longer the angry boy, lashing out, wanting revenge against his family, his life. Her. So why was he here?

Thea didn't let herself believe Helena's theory for a moment. If Zeke had really wanted to see her he'd had eight years. Even if he hadn't wanted to see his family again he could have found her—made contact somehow. But he hadn't. And by the time Thea had known where he was again any lingering regret or wish to see him had long faded. Or at least become too painful to consider. That wound was healed. No point pulling it open again.

Except now he was here, for her wedding, and she didn't have a choice.

Flynn shifted on the seat, switching legs to keep them swinging. 'Anyway… Talking about my prodigal brother isn't going to help you feel any more relaxed about the wedding. Let's talk about more pleasant things.'

'Like?'

'Our honeymoon,' Flynn said decisively, then

faltered. The swing stopped moving and his shoulder grew tense under her cheek. 'I mean… I don't mean…'

Thea smiled against his shirt. He was so *proper*. 'I know what you mean.'

'I was thinking about the day trips we might take—that sort of thing,' Flynn explained unnecessarily. 'There are some very fine vineyards in the region, I believe. I don't want you to think that I'm expecting…well, *anything*. I know that wasn't our agreement.'

Thea pushed herself up to see his face. The agreement. It had been written, signed, notarised months ago—long before the wedding planning had even begun. They both knew what they wanted from this marriage—the business convenience, the companionship, fidelity. The document had addressed the possibility of heirs—and therefore sex—as something to be negotiated in three years' time. That had been Thea's decision. Marriage was one thing. Children were something else altogether. She needed to be sure of her role as a wife first.

But now she wondered if that had been a mistake.

'Maybe we should… I mean, we can talk again about the agreement, if you like?'

Flynn's body stilled further. Then he started the swing moving again, faster than before. 'You've changed your mind?'

'I just…I want our marriage to be solid. I want the companionship, and everything else we discussed, but more than anything I want us to be partners. I don't want doomed passion, or anger and jealousy. I want true friendship and respect, and I know you can give me that.'

'And children?' Flynn asked, and Thea remembered just how important that was to him. How much he needed a family of his own—she suspected not just to make sure there was a legitimate Morrison-Ashton heir for the business.

'In time,' she said, 'yes, I think so. But I'd still like a little time for us to get to know each other better first. You know…as husband and wife.'

Was that enough? Would he get the hint?

'You want us to sleep together?' Flynn said. 'Sorry to be blunt, but I think it's important we both know what we're saying here.'

Another reason he'd make a good husband.

Clarity. She'd never had that with Zeke. Not at all. 'You're right. And, yes, I do.'

'Okay.'

Not exactly the resounding endorsement she'd hoped for. 'Are you all right with that?'

Flynn flashed a smile at her. 'Thea, you're a very beautiful woman and I'm proud that you're going to be my wife. Of course I'm okay with that.'

'You weren't sounding particularly enthusiastic.'

'I am. Really.' He pulled her close again and kissed the top of her head. 'Who knows? Maybe we'll even grow to love each other as more than friends.'

'Perhaps we will,' Thea said. After all, how could she tell her husband-to-be that the last thing she wanted was for either of them to fall in love with each other. Sex, marriage, kids—that was fine. But not love.

Hadn't it been proved, too many times already, that her love wasn't worth enough?

The corridors of the villa were quieter now. Zeke presumed that everyone was lingering over after-dinner drinks in the front parlour or had gone to bed. Either way, he didn't particularly want to join in.

Instead, he made his way to the terrace doors. A little fresh air, a gulp of freedom away from the oppression of family expectation, might do him some good.

Except the terrace was already occupied.

He stood in the doorway for a long moment, watching the couple on the swing. Whatever he'd seen and thought earlier, here—now—they looked like a real couple. Flynn's arm wrapped around Thea's slender shoulders…the kiss he pressed against her head. She had her legs tucked up under her, the way she'd always sat as a teenager, back when they'd spent parties like this hiding out together. The memories were strong: Thea skipping out on her hostessing duties, sipping stolen champagne and talking about the world, confiding in him, telling him her hopes, plans, dreams.

It hurt more than he liked, seeing her share a moment like that with someone else. And for that someone else to be his brother…that burned.

It shouldn't, Zeke knew. He'd moved past the pain of her rejection years ago, and it wasn't as if he hadn't found plenty of solace in other arms.

She'd made her choice eight years ago and he'd lived by it. He hadn't called, hadn't visited. Hadn't given her a chance to change her mind, because he didn't want her to.

She'd chosen their families and he'd chosen himself. Different sides. Love had flared into anger, rejection, even hate. But even hate faded over the years, didn't it? He didn't hate her now. He didn't know what he felt. Not love, for certain. Maybe…regret? A faint, lingering thought that things might have been different.

But they weren't, and Zeke wasn't one for living in the past. Especially not now, when he'd finally made the last cut between himself and his father. He'd turned down the one thing he'd have given anything for as a boy—his father's acceptance and approval. He knew now how little that was worth. He was free, at last.

Except for that small thin thread that kept him tied to the woman on the swing before him. And by the end of the week even that would be gone, when she'd tied herself to another.

His new life would start the moment he left this place. And suddenly he wanted to savour the last few moments of the old one.

Zeke stepped out onto the terrace, a small smile on his lips as his brother looked up and spotted him.

'Zeke,' Flynn said, eyes wary, and Thea's head jerked up from his shoulder.

'I wondered where you two had got to,' Zeke lied. He hadn't given it a moment's thought, because he hadn't imagined they could be like this. *Together*. 'Dinner over, then?'

Thea nodded, sitting up and shifting closer to Flynn to make room for Zeke to sit beside them. 'How did things go? With your father?'

'Pretty much as expected.' Zeke eyed the small space on the swing, then perched on the edge of the low table in front of them instead.

'Which was…?' Flynn sounded a little impatient. 'I don't even know what he wanted to talk to you about. Business, I assume?'

'You didn't tell him?' Zeke asked Thea, eyebrow raised.

'We were talking about more important things,' Thea said, which made Flynn smile softly and kiss her hair again.

Zeke's jaw tightened at the sight. He suspected he didn't want to know what those 'more important things' were. 'Your father wanted to try and buy my business,' he told Flynn.

'He's your father too,' Flynn pointed out.

Zeke laughed. 'Possibly not, after tonight.'

'You told him no, then?' Thea guessed. 'Why? To spite him? You've already admitted you want to sell.'

'He wanted me to come and work for Morrison-Ashton.'

'And that would be the worst thing *ever*, of course.' Sarcasm dripped from her voice. 'Are you really still so angry with him?'

Tilting his head back, Zeke stared up through the slats of the terrace roof at the stars twinkling through. 'No,' he answered honestly. 'This isn't… It's not like it was any more, Thea. I'm not trying to spite him, or hurt him, or pay him back for anything. I just want to move on. Sever all ties and start a whole new life. Maybe a new company, a new field. A new me.'

'So we won't be seeing you again after the wedding, then?' Flynn said, and Zeke realised he'd almost forgotten his brother was even there for a moment. He'd spoken to Thea the same way he'd always talked to Thea—with far more honesty than he'd give anyone else. A bad habit to fall back into.

'Maybe you two would be worth a visit,' he said, forcing a smile. 'After all, I'll need to come and be favourite Uncle Zeke to your kids, right?'

At his words Flynn's expression softened, and he gave his fiancée a meaningful look. Thea, for her part, glanced down at her hands, but Zeke thought he saw a matching shy smile on her face.

Realisation slammed into him, hitting him hard in the chest until he almost gasped for breath. *That* was what they'd been talking about—their 'more important things'. Children. He'd been so sure that this marriage was a sham, that there was nothing between them. But he hadn't imagined kids. Even when he'd made the comment he'd expected an evasion, a convenient practised answer. Another sign that this wasn't real.

Not *this*. Not the image in his head of Thea's belly swollen with his brother's child. Not the thought of how much better parents Flynn and Thea would be than his own father. Of a little girl with Thea's dark hair curling around a perfect face.

'Well, you know you'll always be welcome in our home,' Flynn said.

The words were too formal for brothers, too distant for anything he'd ever shared with Thea. And Zeke knew without a doubt that he'd never, ever be taking them up on the offer. Maybe he didn't love Thea any more, but that tightly stitched line of regret inside him still pulled when she tugged on the thread between them.

He couldn't give Thea what she wanted—never had been able to. She'd made that very clear. And in two days she'd be married, that thread would be cut, and he'd never see her again.

'I should get to bed,' Thea said, unfolding her legs from under her. 'Another long day tomorrow.'

Flynn smiled up at her as she stood. 'I'll see you in the morning?'

Thea nodded, then with a quick glance at Zeke bent and kissed Flynn on the lips. It looked soft, but sure, and Zeke got the message—*loud and clear, thanks*. She'd made her choice—again—and she was sticking with it.

Fine. It was her choice to make, after all. But Zeke knew that the scar of regret would never leave him if he wasn't sure she was happy with the choice she was making. If he wanted the freedom of that cut thread, he had to be able to leave her behind entirely. He had to be sure she knew what she was doing.

Zeke got to his feet. 'I'll walk you to your room.'

CHAPTER FOUR

THIS WAS EXACTLY what she didn't want. Which, in fairness, was probably why Zeke was doing it.

It had been too strange, sitting there with the two brothers, talking about her future as if Zeke might be part of it—in a role she'd simply never expected him to take. Hard enough to transition from fiancée to wife to mother with Flynn, without adding in her ex as her brother-in-law. It had all been so much easier when she'd imagined he was out of her life for good. That she'd never have to see him again. She'd got over the hurt of that loss years before.

The villa was in darkness, and their footsteps echoed off the tiled floors and painted stone walls. The place might be luxurious, but in the moonlight Thea couldn't help but find it creepy. From the hanging tapestries to the stone arches looming overhead, the shadows seemed oppressive. And it felt eerily empty; everyone else must have gone to bed hours before.

She'd expected Zeke to talk, to keep up the banter and the cutting comments and the jokes, but to her surprise they walked in a companionable silence. She could feel him beside her, the warmth of his presence a constant reminder of how close he was. If she stretched out a finger she could reach his hand.

But she wouldn't.

As they climbed the stairs, Zeke only ever one step behind her, his hand next to hers on the banister, she catalogued all the questions she wanted to ask.

Why are you back?

Why didn't you call?

Are you really going to stay?

What do you want from me now?

There had to be a rhyme and reason to it all somewhere, but Thea couldn't quite put her finger on it. Maybe he didn't know the answers, either. Maybe that was why he seemed always on the edge of asking a question he wasn't sure he wanted her to answer.

'I'm just down here,' she whispered as they

reached the top of the stairs. 'You're over that way, right?'

Zeke nodded, but made no effort to head to his own room. After a moment Thea moved towards her door, very aware of him still behind her.

Hand on the door handle, she stopped again. 'What do you want, Zeke?' she asked, looking at the door in front of her.

She felt his sigh, a warm breath against her neck. 'I want to be sure.'

'Sure of what?'

'Sure that you're…happy. That this is really what you want. Before I leave.'

'You're not going to come and visit again, are you?' She'd known that even as he'd talked about being Uncle Zeke. She'd known the truth of it all along. She already knew the answers to all her questions in her heart.

Zeke was here to say goodbye.

'No.'

She turned at the word, and found herself trapped between Zeke's body and the door. He had one arm braced against the wood above her head, the other at his side, fist clenched.

'Why?' More of a breath than a question.

'I need…I need to move on. Away from my family, from yours. For good.'

'Eight years wasn't long enough for you to stop hating us, then?'

'I didn't—'

He stopped short of the lie, which Thea appreciated even as his meaning stabbed her heart. She'd known he hated her. She couldn't let herself be surprised by the confirmation.

'It's not about that any more,' Zeke said instead. He gave a low chuckle. 'I've spent so long caught up in it, in proving myself to my father even as I hated him. So long living my life because of my past, even if I didn't realise I was doing it. And it's time to stop now. Time to build a life for myself, I guess.'

Without us, Thea finished for him in her head.

'So what I need to know is—*are* you happy? Is this really what you want? Or is it just what you think you're supposed to do?'

Zeke's gaze caught hers as he asked his questions, and Thea knew she couldn't look away from those dark eyes even if she'd wanted to.

Was this what she wanted? She thought about Flynn. About how easy it was with him compared to in her previous disastrous attempts at relationships. About everything she could have with him. This wasn't just for their fathers, this time, or even for Helena. This was for her. To give her security, the safety of knowing her place in the world. Knowing where she belonged.

She blinked, and told Zeke, 'This is what I want.'

Time stretched out between them as he stared into her eyes as if scanning for truths. Finally his eyelids fluttered down, and Thea snapped her gaze away.

'Okay...' Zeke spoke softly, and she was sure she heard relief in the word. 'Okay.'

When she looked back he lowered his lips and kissed her, soft and sweet, before stepping away.

'I hope to God you're not lying to me this time, Thea,' he said, and he turned and walked away to his room.

Thea stood and watched him go, the wood of the door at her back and her grip on the door handle the only things holding her up.

'So do I,' she whispered when his door had closed behind him.

* * *

Loosening his tie, Zeke threw himself onto the bed and pulled out his phone. He'd promised Deb an update when he arrived, but between Thea in her underwear and thwarting his father he hadn't had much of a chance.

He checked his watch; London was behind them anyway. She'd still be up.

'So?' Deb said when she answered. Her usual greetings and pleasantries were apparently not deemed necessary for him. 'How's it going?'

'My father wants to buy This Minute.'

'He heard we were selling to Glasshouse?' Deb asked, but there didn't seem to be much of a question in her words. More of a sense of inevitability.

Suspicion flared up. 'Yeah. Any idea how that might have happened?'

'Not a clue,' she replied easily. 'But it's kind of handy, don't you think?'

'No.' Had she leaked it? Why? He should be mad, he supposed, but he trusted Deb. She always had a perfectly logical reason for her actions, and he was kind of curious to find out what it was this time.

'I do,' she said. 'I mean, with two interested parties the price will go up, for starters. And, more than that, this gives you a chance to decide what you really want.'

'Other than to get out of here?'

'That's one option,' Deb said. 'The other is to return to the family fold.'

Zeke remembered the look on his father's face when he'd turned him down. That had felt good. 'I think I already burnt that bridge tonight.'

'That works too.' Deb sounded philosophical about the whole thing. 'At least it was your choice to make this time.'

Sometimes Zeke really regretted the occasional late-night drinking sessions with his business partner. His tongue got loose after alcohol, and she knew him far too well as a result.

'Anyway, it's done,' he said, steamrollering past any analysis of his relationship with his father that she had planned. 'Now I just need to get through the wedding and then I can get back to my real life again.'

'Ah, yes. "The Wedding".' Her tone made it very clear that it had capital letters.

'That is what I came here for.'

'And how was it? Seeing Thea again?'

A vision of her standing there, wedding dress around her waist, flooded his mind. But Deb really didn't need to know about that. 'Fine.'

'You think she really wants to marry your brother?'

'I do.' He was just unsure about her motives.

'Then do you really have to stay?'

'I'm the best man, Deb. Kinda necessary to the proceedings.'

'Zeke…' Her voice was serious now, and he knew it was time to stop joking.

'It's fine. It's just a couple of days and I can put it all behind me.'

'You don't have to put yourself through this, you know. If you're satisfied that she's not being coerced into this by your father—'

'Oh, I'm pretty sure she is.'

'But you said—'

'Which doesn't mean she doesn't want to go through with it.' He sighed. Explaining the peculiarities of the Morrison and Ashton families to outsiders was never easy. 'Look, I need to stay. I need to see this through. It's the only way I'm ever going to…I don't know.'

'Have closure?' Deb said, knowing his own

thoughts better than himself as usual. That was always disturbing. 'Fine. But if you need me to manufacture a work emergency to get you out of there...'

'I know where you are. Thanks, Deb.'

'Any time.' She paused, and he got the impression she wasn't quite done with him yet. 'Just... don't stay just to punish yourself, okay?'

'Punish myself for what?'

'Leaving her in the first place.'

The phone went dead in his hand. Apparently goodbyes were no longer necessary, either. He tossed it onto the bedside table and flopped back onto the bed.

This time Deb didn't know what she was talking about. Zeke had absolutely nothing to feel sorry for.

He just hoped Thea knew that, too.

Thea didn't sleep.

She dotted concealer under her eyes the next morning, knowing that Helena would spot the dark shadows anyway. She'd just have to tell her that it was pre-wedding nerves. Which would no doubt lead to another rousing rendition of the *'It's not too late to back out'* chorus. Still, that had to be better than telling her sister the truth.

The truth about the past, that was. Thea wasn't even sure if *she* understood the truth of her and Zeke in the present.

Helena had laid out her chosen outfit for Thea to wear the day before her wedding and Thea slipped into the pale linen dress without question. One of the advantages of having a younger sister with an eye for style, colour and fashion was never having to worry if she'd chosen the right outfit for an occasion. This week, more than ever, she needed the boost to her confidence of knowing she looked good.

She appreciated it even more when, as she reached the bottom of the stairs, she was accosted by Ezekiel Ashton, Senior.

'Thea! Excellent. I just need a little word with you, if you wouldn't mind.'

Whether she minded or not, Ezekiel ushered Thea into his temporary office—away from the tempting smells of hot coffee and pastries.

Ezekiel's desk was covered in papers and files, his laptop pushed away to the corner, precariously balanced on a stack of books. Thea cleared a ream of paper covered in numbers from the visitor's chair and sat down. His office at the company headquarters was usually neat to the point of anal. Had he been up all night working after his meeting with Zeke? Or was he just missing his terrifyingly efficient PA Dorothy? And, either way, what exactly did he think he needed Thea for?

What if this wasn't business? What if this was some sort of *'welcome to the family, don't hurt my son'* talk? And, if so, how could she be sure which son? Because he was a little late for one of them…

Laughter bubbled up in her chest and Thea swallowed it down as Ezekiel creakily lowered himself into his chair. This was Ezekiel Ashton. Of course it was going to be about business.

'Now, Thea. I appreciate that work might not be your highest priority today, given your imminent nuptials. But this wedding has given us a unique opportunity. One I need you to take full advantage of.'

He gave her a meaningful look across the desk, and Thea's heart sank. This was business, yes, but it was personal, too. This was about Zeke.

'What are you hoping I'll be able to do?' Thea

crossed her legs and stared back at her father-in-law-to-be. She couldn't promise anything when it came to Zeke. She'd burnt that bridge long ago. But how to explain that to Ezekiel without telling the whole miserable story?

Ezekiel leant back in his chair, studying her. 'Zeke has always been…fond of you.'

He waited, as if for confirmation, and Thea forced a nod.

'We were friends. When we were younger.'

'I'm hoping you might be able to utilise that friendship.'

No sugarcoating it, then. Not that she'd really expected any such thing from Ezekiel.

'We haven't seen each other in eight years,' Thea pointed out. 'And we didn't…we weren't on the best of terms when he left.'

A slightly raised eyebrow was the only hint that this came as a surprise to Zeke's father. 'Still. After all this time I'm sure you can both forgive and forget.'

Forgive? Thea thought she'd managed that years ago, until Zeke had shown up and reminded her of all the reasons she had to be angry with him. Almost as many as he had to be angry with her.

Forget? Never.

Thea took a breath. Time to refocus the conversation. 'This is about This Minute, right?'

Ezekiel gave a sharp nod. 'I'm sure you can understand the value to Morrison-Ashton of bringing Zeke's little business under the company umbrella.'

'I'd hardly call it a "little business",' Thea said. Its turnover figures for last year had been astronomical. Far higher than their own digital news arm. 'And I think the detrimental effect of *not* buying This Minute is of far higher importance to you.'

'True.'

His gaze held a hint of grudging appreciation. *Good*. In her five years working her way up to running the PR department of Morrison-Ashton Ezekiel had never given her a single sign that he appreciated the work she did, or believed it really added value to the company. It was about time he realised she brought more than a name and some money to the table. She wasn't her father, after all.

'Which is why I need you to persuade him to sell This Minute to us,' Ezekiel finished.

Any satisfaction Thea had felt flew away. *Why*

did he have to choose this day to suddenly have faith in my abilities?

'I was under the impression that Zeke had already declined your offer.' And he would continue to do so. She might not have seen him in eight years, but she knew Zeke. He'd never give his father what he wanted without a fight.

'Of course he has,' Ezekiel said, impatiently. 'Otherwise why would I need you? Zeke's letting his pride get in the way, as usual. He knows that the best thing for him and This Minute is to become part of Morrison-Ashton, and for him to take up his rightful role here.'

The role you refused to give him eight years ago. 'He seems very set on moving on to something new.'

'And selling This Minute to Glasshouse.'

'Glasshouse?'

That would be a disaster. For Morrison-Ashton, at least. This Minute would give their main competitor a huge advantage in the digital arena, and the PR fallout from Zeke Ashton defecting to Glasshouse would run and run. It would certainly eclipse any positive coverage her wedding to Flynn was likely to garner.

'Precisely,' Ezekiel said, as if he'd heard every one of her thoughts. 'We need Zeke to sell to Morrison-Ashton. For the family as much as the business. So, you'll do it?'

Could she? Would Zeke listen to her? Would he care? Or would he go out of his way to do the opposite of anything she asked, just as he did with his father? If she could make him see reason…if she could win this for them… This wouldn't just be a business victory. This would assure her place in the Ashton family more than marrying Flynn could achieve.

But even if he did listen…could she ask this of him? Could she choose the business and the family over Zeke all over again, knowing it would hurt him?

Only one way to find out.

'I'll do it.'

Zeke had never given very much thought to weddings beyond showing up in an appropriate suit and whether or not there'd be a free bar. But sitting at a small wrought-iron table at the edge of the villa's huge entrance hall, taking his time over coffee, he had to conclude that, really, weddings were a whole lot of palaver.

The villa had been humming with activity since dawn, as far as he could tell. Before he'd even made it downstairs garlands of flowers and vines had been twisted round the banisters of the staircase, the floors had been polished, and potted trees with ribbons tied around their trunks had been placed at the base of each arch that spanned the hall.

He had no doubt that every other room in the villa would be receiving similar treatment over the next twenty-four hours, but they'd started with the area most likely to be seen by the greatest number of people that day.

And, boy, were there a lot of people. Guests had started arriving very early that morning, flying in from all over the world. From his chosen seat he had a great view of the front door, through a large arch that opened onto the hallway. Clearly not everyone was staying at the hotel down the road, as several couples and families with suitcases had pitched up already and been shown to their rooms. Family, Zeke supposed. He recognised some and recognised the looks he received even better. First the double-take, checking that it really was him. Then the raised eyebrows. Then a whisper to a companion and the whole thing started over again.

Zeke had seriously considered, more than once, taking a pen to the linen napkin he'd been given and fashioning some sort of sign.

Yes, it would say, *it really is me. Zeke Ashton Junior, black sheep, passed-over heir, broke his mother's heart and had the cheek to come back for his brother's wedding. And, no, I'm not selling my father my company, either. Shocking, isn't it?*

The only thing that stopped him was that, even if he managed to fit all that on a napkin, no one would be able to read it from the sort of distance they were keeping. So instead he smiled politely, raised his coffee cup, and refused point-blank to leave his table. People wanted to stare? Let them.

As the hour became more reasonable other people started to stop by, ostensibly to drop off presents but probably to gawp at the villa and try and catch a glimpse of the bride. Zeke wished them luck; he hadn't seen hide nor hair of her since he'd said goodnight the evening before.

That, Zeke thought ruefully, had been a mistake.

Swilling the dregs of his coffee around at the bottom of his cup, he tried not to remember the way Thea had smelled, so close in the darkness, and failed. Just as he'd failed to forget every moment of that last night he'd spent with her before he left.

The way she'd smiled at him before the party. The way she'd kissed him and sworn that it didn't matter when he told her about Flynn taking his job. The way she'd supported him when he'd decided to go and face his father, tell him what he really thought of him.

How his rage had bubbled to the surface as he'd approached his father's office. How unprepared he'd been for what he'd heard there.

Mostly he remembered the moment he'd known he had to leave. Right then—that night. He remembered climbing up to Thea's window to ask her to come with him, and her tears as she told him she couldn't. Wouldn't. The way his heart had stung as he'd realised she really meant it.

Eight years and he couldn't shake that memory.

Couldn't shake the hurt, either.

Catching the eye of the maid, Zeke gave her his most charming smile. She frowned, but headed off to fetch the coffee carafe anyway. Zeke supposed she had other things she was supposed to be doing today, and he was stopping her. But no one had told *him* what to do. He might be the best man, but it seemed the title was wholly ceremonial. Flynn had disappeared out earlier with one of their cousins, apparently not even spotting Zeke at his table. Whatever tasks there were to be performed today, Flynn seemed to have plenty of help.

Which left him here, drinking too much coffee, and overthinking things. Not ideal.

Across the wide hallway he heard heels clicking on stone and looked up, already knowing somehow who it was.

Thea looked tired, Zeke thought. Was that his fault? Had she been kept awake thinking about exactly where everything had gone wrong between them as he had? He motioned to the maid for a second coffee cup and waited for Thea to cross the hall and sit down at his table. Even if she wanted to avoid him he knew the lure of coffee would be too strong for her.

It took her a while, because another crowd of people had arrived with gifts wrapped in silver paper and too much ribbon and she'd got caught up playing hostess. Zeke watched her smiling and welcoming and thanking and thought she looked even less like the girl he remembered than she had in her wedding dress. The Thea he'd known had hated this—all the fake smiles and pretending to be delighted by the third set of champagne flutes to arrive in the last half-hour. She'd played the part well enough after her mother died, at her father's insistence, the same way she'd acted as a mother to Helena and run the Morrison household for the three of them. But she'd always escaped away upstairs at Morrison-Ashton company parties, as soon as it was at all polite. These days it seemed she relished playing the part.

Eventually Isabella arrived, her smiles and gestures even bigger than Thea's. As his mother took over the meet-and-greet, Thea stepped back from her guests, a slightly disappointed frown settling onto her forehead, looking suddenly out of place. After a moment she moved across the hallway towards him. And the coffee. Zeke had no doubt that the caffeine was more appealing to her than his presence.

'Good morning, Zeke.' Thea swept her skirt under her as she sat, and smiled her thanks at the maid as she poured the coffee. 'Did you sleep well?'

'Like a baby,' Zeke lied. 'And yourself?'

'Fine, thank you.'

'Up early on wedding business?' he asked, waving his coffee cup in the direction of the new arrivals.

'Actually, I was just catching up on a few work things before tomorrow.' Thea picked up her cup and blew across the surface. 'I'll be off for almost a month for the honeymoon, so I'm trying to make sure everything is properly handed over.'

'I'd have thought you'd have more important things to do today than work. Wedding things,' he added when she looked confused.

Thea glanced down at her coffee cup again. 'To be honest, I've been able to leave most of that to the wedding planner. And Helena and Flynn.'

'Most brides *want* to be involved in their wedding plans, you know.' At least, the ones who wanted to get married. Who were marrying a man they loved. And Zeke was beginning to think that Thea didn't fall into *either* of those categories, whatever she said.

'I didn't say I haven't been involved,' Thea said,

her voice sharp. 'But at this point it's all the last-minute details and fiddly bits, and Helena is much better at making things look good than I am.'

'So, what *are* you doing today, then?' Zeke asked.

'Actually, I do have one very important wedding-related task to do,' Thea said. 'And I could really use your help.'

Zeke raised his eyebrows. 'Oh?'

Thea nodded. 'I need to buy Flynn a groom's gift. I thought you might be able to help me find something he'd like.'

He hadn't seen his brother in eight years, and he'd had precious little clue what the man liked before then. But if this was the excuse Thea needed to talk to him about whatever was really on her mind, he'd play along. It might even be fun.

'Okay,' he said, draining his coffee. 'I'll bring my car round while you get ready to go.'

But Thea shook her head. 'Oh, no. *I'm* driving.'

CHAPTER FIVE

THE MORE SHE thought about it, the more Thea was convinced that this was a brilliant idea. She could use the shopping trip to sound Zeke out on his plans for This Minute before she approached the more difficult task of convincing him to sell it to Morrison-Ashton. And at the same time she could prove exactly how happy she was to be marrying Flynn by choosing her husband-to-be the perfect wedding gift.

Plus, it got her out of the villa—*and* she got to drive. That was almost enough to assuage the twinges of guilt that still plagued her about her mission that morning.

'Why am I not surprised?' Zeke asked as she pulled up outside the front door in her little red convertible.

'I like to drive.' Thea shrugged, her hands never leaving the wheel as Zeke opened the passenger door and lowered himself into the seat. 'It was an engagement present from Flynn.'

Well, he'd given it to her anyway. She rather suspected that Helena had helped him choose it. Flynn's idea of appropriate gifts tended to be more along the line of whatever the jeweller recommended.

'Of course it was.' Zeke buckled up his seat belt and rested his arm along the side of the door.

He looked casual enough, but Thea knew he was gripping the seat with his other hand. He'd complained regularly about her driving in the eleven months between her passing her test and him leaving.

'So, where are we going?'

'There's a small town just twenty minutes' drive or so away.' Smoothly, Thea pulled away from the villa and headed down the driveway, picking up speed as they passed another load of guests coming up. She'd just have to pretend she hadn't seen them later. 'It has some nice little shops, and there's a wonderful trattoria where we can stop for lunch.'

'Sounds nice. And I'm honoured that you're

choosing to spend your last day of single life with me. Really.'

Thea rolled her eyes and ignored him. There was plenty of time to deal with Zeke and his terrible sense of what counted as funny once they reached the town. For now, she just wanted to enjoy the drive.

Zeke fiddled with the car stereo as Thea turned off onto the main road, and soon they were flying through the gentle hills and green and yellow fields of the Tuscan countryside to the sound of the classic rock music he'd always insisted on.

'I *know* I don't own this CD,' Thea said—not that she cared. Somehow it sounded right. As if they'd fallen back in time to the day she'd passed her driving test, just a few weeks after her seventeenth birthday, and Zeke had let her drive his car for the first time.

Zeke held up his phone, connected to the stereo by a lead she hadn't known existed. 'You know me. I never travel without a proper soundtrack.'

The summer sun beamed down on them as they drove along the winding road, past farms and other villas and the occasional vineyard. She'd have two weeks to explore this land with Flynn,

Thea thought. Two whole weeks to get used to the idea of being his wife, to get to know him as her husband, before they headed back to London to set up their new home together. It would be perfect.

The heat on her shoulders relaxed her muscles and she realised that Zeke was blissfully silent beside her, not even commenting on her speed, as any other passenger might have done. Maybe he was remembering that first trip out, too. Maybe he was remembering what had happened afterwards, when they'd found a ruined barn on the edge of a nearby farm and he'd spread his jacket out over the hay as he laid her down and kissed her...

Thea glanced at the speedometer and relaxed her foot off the accelerator just a touch.

Time to think of calmer things. Like Flynn, and their honeymoon.

Eventually she slowed down to something approaching the speed limit as they passed rows of stone houses on the outskirts and joined the other traffic heading over the bridge into the town. Thea pulled into the same parking space she'd used the last time she'd visited, just outside the main *piazza*. She grabbed her handbag, waiting for Zeke to get out before she locked the car.

'So,' he asked, pushing his sunglasses up onto his head as he stepped into the shade of the nearest building, 'where first?'

Thea stared down the street, through its red stone arches and paving, and realised she hadn't a clue. What *did* you buy your future husband as a wedding gift, anyway? Especially one who, even after decades of friendship, you didn't actually know all that well?

Glinting glass caught her eye, and she remembered the jeweller's and watch shop she and Helena had found down a winding side street off the *piazza*. Surely there'd be something there?

'This way,' she said, striding in what she hoped was the right direction through the crowds gathered to watch a street entertainer in the *piazza*.

'Where you lead...' Zeke said easily, letting her pass before falling into step with her.

Thea's stride faltered just for a moment. He didn't mean anything by it, she was sure—probably didn't even remember the song. But at his words a half-forgotten melody lodged in her head, playing over and over. A promise to always follow, no matter what.

Her mum had sung it often, before she died. And Thea remembered singing along. The tune was as much a part of her childhood as bickering with Helena over hairbands and party shoes. But more than that she remembered singing it to Zeke, late at night, after half a bottle of champagne smuggled upstairs from the party below. Remembered believing, for a time, that it was true. That she'd follow him anywhere.

Until he'd actually asked her to leave with him.

Shaking her head to try and dislodge the memory, she realised they were there and pushed open the shop door. There was no time for dwelling on ancient history now. She was getting married tomorrow.

And she still needed to find her groom the perfect gift.

'Right,' she said. 'Let's see what this place has that screams *Flynn*.'

The answer, Zeke decided pretty quickly, was not much.

While Thea examined racks of expensive

watches and too flashy cufflinks he trailed his fingers over the glass cases and looked around at the other stuff. Flynn wasn't a flashy cufflinks kind of guy, as far as he remembered. But maybe Thea knew better these days.

He glanced over and she held up a gold watch, its oversized face flashing in the bright overhead lights. 'What about this?'

'Flynn has a watch,' Zeke pointed out.

'Yeah, but maybe he'd like a new one. From his wife.'

'Wife-to-be. And I doubt it. The one he wears was Grandad's.' He'd spotted it on his brother's wrist the night before, at dinner, and stamped down on the memory of the day their father had given it to him.

'Oh.' Thea handed the watch back to the assistant. 'Maybe we'll look at the cufflinks instead, then.'

With a sigh, Zeke turned back to the other cases, filled with precious gems and metals. Maybe he should get something for his mother. Something sparkly would probably be enough to make up for any of the apparent pain Thomas had said she'd felt at his departure. Not that Zeke had seen any actual evidence of that pain.

Maybe she was just too caught up in the wedding festivities to remember that she'd missed him. It wouldn't be the first time that other people, other events, had taken precedence over her own sons.

A necklace caught Zeke's eye: pale gold with a bright blue sapphire at the centre. The same colour as Thea's dress the night before. He could almost imagine himself fastening it around her neck as they stood outside her room—a sign that he still... what? Cared? Remembered what they'd had? Regretted how things had ended? Wanted her to be happy? Knew that even though they'd both moved on they'd always be part of each other's past?

That was the hardest thing, he decided. Not even knowing what he wanted to tell Thea, what he needed her to understand. It wasn't as simple as hating her—it never could be, with Thea. But it wasn't as if he'd shown up here this weekend to tell her not to marry Flynn, to run away with him at last instead. As they should have done eight years ago.

No, what he felt for Thea was infinitely more

complicated. And if there was a single piece of jewellery that could convey it to her, without him having to find the words, he'd buy it for her in a heartbeat—no matter the cost. But there wasn't.

With a sigh, Zeke dragged his gaze to the next case, only to find tray after tray of sparkling diamond solitaires glinting up at him.

Engagement rings. *Not helpful, universe. And why choose now to get a sense of humour, huh?*

Besides, she already had one of those. He'd glimpsed it flashing in the candlelight at dinner, recognising it as his grandmother's, and had barely even managed to muster any surprise about it. What else would the favoured Ashton heir give to his fiancé-cum-business partner? They were building an empire together, based on their joint family history.

A history Zeke had all but been written out of eight years ago.

'I'm going to have to think about it,' Thea told the shop assistant apologetically, and Zeke, realising he was still staring at the engagement rings, spun round to face her.

'We're leaving?'

'For now,' Thea said.

Zeke followed her out of the shop, letting the door swing shut behind him. 'Nothing that screamed *Flynn*, huh?'

'Not really. He's not really a flashy cufflinks kind of guy, is he?'

Something tightened in Zeke's chest, hearing her echo his thoughts, but he couldn't say if it was because she knew Flynn better than he'd thought or because her thought processes still so closely resembled his.

'So, where next?' he asked, trying to ignore the feeling.

'Um, there's a leather shop down here somewhere.' She waved her hand into an arcade of small, dark but probably insanely expensive shops, hidden under the arched stone roof. She hadn't even let Helena explore them properly last time. 'Do you think Flynn needs a new briefcase?'

'I think Flynn will love whatever you buy him, because it's from you.'

Thea gave him a look. One that suggested she was trying to evaluate if he might have been taken over by aliens recently. 'Seriously?'

'Okay, I think he'll pretend to love it, whatever it is, because that's the appropriate thing to do.'

'And Flynn *does* like appropriate.' She sighed and headed towards the leather shop anyway. 'Do you remember the hideous tie you bought him that last summer?'

'He wore it for his first day at work,' Zeke said, relishing the thought all over again. It had been the most truly horrendous tie he'd been able to find anywhere. Expensive, of course, so that his mother couldn't object. But hugely inappropriate for the serious workplace with its neon tartan. The perfect graduation gift for the perfect brother. Zeke had known Flynn would wear it just so as not to offend him. And that Flynn would never realise it was a joke gift.

'He changed it on the train before going into the office,' Thea told him, thus ruining a perfect memory.

'Seriously? That's a shame. I did love thinking of him sitting in meetings with the board wearing that tie,' Zeke said wistfully.

'He's probably still got it somewhere,' Thea said. 'He might not be stupid enough to wear it for work, but he's definitely sentimental enough that he won't have thrown it away. After all, it was the last thing you gave him before…'

'Before I left,' Zeke finished for her. 'Yeah, I don't think he was as bothered by that as you think.' Seemed like nobody had been.

She gave him a small sad smile. 'Then maybe I do know your brother better than you, after all.'

Did she? She should—she was marrying the guy. But the very fact she'd admitted she wasn't sure that she did... The contradictions buzzed around Zeke's brain, and at the heart of them was the disturbing thought that maybe Flynn *had* cared after all.

And another question. Had Thea?

The problem, Thea decided, wasn't that she didn't *know* what sort of things Flynn liked. It was just that he knew them better and had, in pretty much every case, provided them for himself. He already had the perfect briefcase, his grandfather's watch and a reliable pair of cufflinks. Whatever the item, he'd have researched it, chosen the best-quality one he required, and been satisfied with his purchase. Whatever she bought would be used a few times, to show his appreciation, then shoved to the back of a cupboard like that hideous neon tartan joke tie.

This whole trip had been a mistake. She'd wanted to show Zeke that she knew her fiancé, that they were in tune as a couple. Instead all she seemed to be proving was that whatever she brought to the marriage wasn't really required.

No. This wasn't about briefcases and watches. She brought a lot more to the table than material goods. She wasn't her father, just providing the money and then sitting back to watch the tide of success come rolling in. She was part of the company, part of Flynn's life, and part of their future together.

Which was great as a pep talk, but rubbish at helping her find a wedding present for her husband-to-be.

'What about this one?' Zeke held up a tan leather handbag. 'It's a man bag!'

'I'm pretty sure it's not,' Thea said. 'It has flowers decorating the strap.'

'Flynn's secure enough in his masculinity to carry it off,' Zeke argued, slinging the bag over his shoulder and pouting like a male model.

'I am *not* buying him the wedding present equivalent of a neon tartan tie, Zeke.' Thea turned back to the briefcases and heard him sigh behind her.

'Then what *are* you going to buy him?' Zeke picked up a black briefcase and flipped the latch open. 'Hasn't he already got one of these?'

'Yes.'

'So does he need a new one?'

'No.'

'Then can we go for lunch?'

Thea sighed. He did have a point, and she *was* hungry. She'd missed breakfast, thanks to Ezekiel Senior and his request.

She tensed at the memory. Never mind the perfect wedding gift, she had another job to do today. And lunch would be the perfect time to broach the subject. Preferably after Zeke had enjoyed a glass or two of wine. Or three. Three might be the magic number.

'Come on, then,' she said, opening the door and preparing to leave the cool shadows of the shopping arcade behind and step back out into the piazza. She waved a hand in the direction of a familiar-looking dark alleyway. 'The little trattoria I was talking about is down here somewhere.'

It wasn't fancy, but Zeke had never been one for the expensive restaurants and big-name places. He'd used to prefer hidden gems and secret spots that were just their own. She was always surprised, even after so long, when she caught a magazine photo of him at some celebrity chef's opening night at a new restaurant, or on the red carpet with some actress or another. That wasn't the Zeke she remembered. And now, spending time with him again, she wondered if it was even the Zeke he'd become. Was it just that being seen was the only way he had to let his father know that he was a success now, in his own right?

Maybe she'd ask him. After the wedding. And after she'd persuaded him to sell This Minute to his father.

So probably never, then.

Thea pushed open the heavy painted wood door under a sign that just read 'Trattoria' and let Zeke in first. He smiled at the nearest waitress and she found them a table next to the window without hesitation; only a few other tables were occupied. Thea couldn't help but think this was probably a good thing. If Zeke threw pasta all over her when she tried to talk to him about his father at least there wouldn't be too many witnesses. Helena would be cross about the dress, though…

'Can I get you some drinks?' the waitress asked,

her English clearly far better than Thea's Italian had ever been. She let Zeke order a local beer before she asked for a soft drink. Alcohol really wasn't going to help the conversation they needed to have.

'So, you've been here before?' Zeke asked, looking around him at the faded pictures on the stone walls and the bare wooden tables.

The small windows had all been thrown open to let in air, but the heat of the day and the lack of breeze meant that not much coolness was moving around, save from the lazy spin of the lone ceiling fan. Thea's dress had started to stick to her back already, and she longed for that soft drink.

'I came here with Helena last week,' she said. 'Just after we arrived. I can recommend the *pappardelle* with wild boar sauce.'

'With Helena? Not Flynn?' Zeke pressed.

Thea wondered why he cared anyway. He'd left, and had every intention of leaving again, without even the faint hope that he might return this time. What did he care if she married Flynn or not? Besides not letting his brother win, of course.

Maybe that was what this came down to. All Zeke wanted was to prove a point and then he'd move on. In which case she had pretty much no chance of talking him into selling them This Minute.

But she still had to try.

'No, not with Flynn. He didn't fly in until a couple of days ago. They needed him in the office.'

'But they didn't need you?'

Dammit. Why did Zeke always know exactly what niggled at her? And why did he always have to push at that point?

'My planning for the wedding kind of *is* part of my job at the moment.' Thea toyed with the menu in her hand so she didn't have to see his reaction to that.

'Of course,' Zeke said. 'The final union of the two biggest families in media. It's quite the PR stunt.'

'It's also my life,' Thea snapped back.

'Yeah, but after the last twenty-four hours I still can't tell which of those is more important to you.'

Thea looked up, searching for a response to that one, and gave an inward sigh of relief when she saw the waitress coming over with their drinks.

'Are you ready to order?' she asked, placing the glasses on the table.

Zeke smiled at her—that charming, happy-go-lucky smile he never gave Thea any more. 'I'll have the wild boar *pappardelle*, please. I hear it's excellent.'

'The same, please,' Thea said. But she wasn't thinking about food. She was thinking about how she'd let her work become her life, and let her life drift away entirely.

Zeke sipped his beer and watched Thea, lost in thought across the table. He'd thought it would be fun, needling her about how her wedding was actually work. He'd had a run of honeymoon jokes lined up in his head—ones he knew she'd hate. But now...well, the humour had gone.

'I'm sorry,' he said, even though he wasn't sure he was, really. He'd only told the truth, after all. Something that happened far too little in their families.

'You're *sorry*?' Thea asked disbelievingly.

Zeke shrugged. 'Not really the done thing, is it? Upsetting the bride the day before her wedding.'

'I'm not upset.'

'Are you sure? Because you look a little...

blotchy.' The way she always had moments before she started crying.

But Thea shook her head, reaching for her glass with a steady hand. 'I'm fine. Like you say, you've been back less than twenty-four hours. I don't expect you to understand the relationship and the agreement that Flynn and I have developed and nurtured over the past two years.'

'Two years? You've been with him that long?'

'Yes. You don't think marriage is something I'd rush into, do you?'

Actually, he'd assumed that the idea had come up in a board meeting, that their respective fathers had put forward a proposal document to each of them and they'd weighed up the pros and cons before booking the church. But Zeke didn't think she'd appreciate *that* analysis.

'You did last time,' he said instead. 'With What's-his-name.'

'Cameron,' she supplied. 'And how did you know about him?'

'I wasn't thinking about him.' How many guys *had* she almost married since he'd left? 'I meant the Canadian.'

'Scott.'

'Yeah. I read about him on our Canadian news site. Hockey player, right?'

'Right.'

'Whirlwind engagement, I heard.'

'And he was equally quick with the cheating, as it turned out.'

'Ah.' He hadn't known that. All that had been reported was that the wedding had been called off with hours to spare. So like Thea to protect the guy's reputation even as he was hurting her. 'So who was this Cameron guy, then?'

'A business associate. Turned out he loved my business, and my money, a lot more than he loved me.'

'Never mix business with pleasure, huh?' Zeke said, before remembering that that was exactly what she was doing with Flynn. 'I mean...'

Thea sighed. 'Don't worry. I am well aware of the disastrous reputation of my love-life. You can't say anything I haven't heard before.'

He hated seeing her like this. So certain she would make a mistake. Was that why she was marrying Flynn? The safest bet in a world full of potential mistakes?

'Sometimes a woman has to choose the safest

road, Zeke. We can't all afford to hike the harder trails if we want to arrive safely.' The words were his mother's, eight years old now, but he could see their truth in Thea's face. For the first time he wondered who Thea would have become if her own mother had lived. Or if Thomas Morrison had never met Ezekiel Ashton. Would she be happier? Probably, he decided.

'You weren't always rubbish at love,' Zeke said, the words coming out soft and low.

Her gaze flashed up to meet him, as if she was looking for a hidden jibe or more mockery. He tried to keep his expression clear, to show her that all he meant was the words he'd said.

Clearly he failed. 'Yeah, right. Funny man. Of course you know *exactly* how early my failure at love started.'

'I didn't mean—' he started, but she cut him off.

'My first love—you—climbed out of a window to escape from me on my eighteenth birthday, Zeke. I think we can all see where the pattern started.' Bitterness oozed out of her voice, but all Zeke could hear was her saying, *'No, Zeke. I can't.'* Eight years and the sound had never left him.

Hang on. 'Wait. Are you blaming *me* for your

unlucky love-life?' Because as far as he was concerned he was the one who should be assigning blame here.

'No. Yes. Maybe.' She twisted her napkin in her hands, wrapping it round her fingers then letting it go again.

'I feel much better for that clarification.'

'I don't want to talk about this any more.'

She might not, but after eight years Zeke had some things he wanted to say. And she was bloody well going to listen. 'And, in the name of accuracy, I wasn't trying to escape you. In fact you might recall me begging you to come with me.' Standing on that stupid wobbly trellis, wrecking whatever that purple flower had been, clinging onto the windowsill. She'd looked out at him, all dark hair and big eyes, and broken his heart.

'I wouldn't call it begging,' Thea said, but even she didn't sound convinced.

'You said no. You chose to stay. You can't blame me for that.' That moment—that one moment— had changed his entire life. Made him the person he was today. She could at least *try* to remember it right.

'You chose to leave me. So why can't I blame you? You're still blaming me. Isn't that why you're here? To make my life miserable because I made the right decision eight years ago and you hate that I was right for once?'

No. That wasn't it. That wasn't what he was doing. He was here to draw a line under everything there had ever been between them, under his bitter resentment of his family that had ruled his life for too long. Zeke was moving on.

But sometimes moving on required looking backwards. Closure—that was what this was.

'The right decision,' she'd said. 'You never once imagined what life might have been like if you' d left with me that night?' Because he had driven himself crazy with it even when he'd known it was pointless. Self-destructive, even. Had she been spared that?

Apparently not. 'Of course I did, Zeke! Endlessly, and a thousand different ways. But it doesn't change the fact that I was needed at home. That I was right to stay.'

And suddenly Zeke knew what it was he needed

to move on. What it would take to get the closure he craved.

So he looked up at her and asked the question. 'Why?'

CHAPTER SIX

WHY?

As if that wasn't a question she'd asked herself a million times over the past eight years.

She knew the answer, of course. Helena. She'd needed a big sister right then, more than ever. Thea couldn't have left her, and she didn't regret staying for her for one moment.

But if she was honest that wasn't the only answer. And it wasn't the one she wanted to give Zeke. It wasn't her secret to tell, apart from anything else.

'Because we were too young. Too stupid. Zeke, I was barely eighteen, and you were asking me to leave my whole life behind. My family, my future, my plans and dreams. My place in the world. Everything.'

'I'd have been your family. Your place. Your future.'

Zeke stared at her, his face open and honest. For

the first time since he'd come back Thea thought she might be seeing the boy she'd known behind the man he'd become.

'You know I'd have moved mountains to give you anything you wanted. To make every dream you had come true.'

The worst part was she did know that. Had known it even then. But she hadn't been able to take the risk.

'Perhaps. But, successful as you are now, I bet it wasn't like that to start with. You'd have had to struggle, work every hour there was, take risks with your money, your reputation.' She could see from his face it was true. 'And what did you think I'd be doing while you were doing that? I wanted to go to university, Zeke. I had my place—all ready and waiting. I didn't want to give that up to keep house for you while you chased your dream.'

'I wouldn't… It wouldn't have been like that.'

'Wouldn't it?'

'No.' He sounded firmer this time. 'Look, I can't change the past, and I can't say what would have happened. But, Thea, you know me. *Knew* me, at least. And you have to know I would never have asked you to give up your dreams for mine.'

'Sorry…' the waitress said, lowering their plates to the table. 'I didn't mean to… Enjoy!'

She scampered off towards the kitchen and Thea wondered how much she'd heard. How much she was now retelling to the restaurant staff.

Zeke hadn't even looked at his lunch. 'Tell me you know that, Thea. I wouldn't have done that.'

Thea loaded pasta onto her fork. 'Maybe you wouldn't. Not intentionally. But it happens.' She'd seen it happen to too many friends, after they got married or when they started a family. At eighteen, she didn't think she'd have had the self-awareness to fight it.

'What about now, then?' Zeke asked, still looking a little shaken. 'Do you really think it will be different with Flynn?'

'Yes,' Thea said, without hesitation. She knew about business—knew what she needed to do there. Her marriage with Flynn would only enhance that. She wouldn't give it up just to be someone's wife. 'We've talked about it. About our future. We both know what we're getting into.'

Had it all written down in legalese, ready to be signed along with the marriage register.

Their conversation on the terrace the night before came back to her and she felt a jangle of nerves and excitement when she thought about what she'd agreed to now. Maybe that—a family—would be what she needed to make the whole thing feel real. She knew it was what Flynn wanted, after all. She frowned. But they hadn't spoken yet about what would happen then. Would he expect her to stay at home and look after the kids? If so, they had a problem.

Mentally, she added the topic to the list of honeymoon discussions to have. They had time. They hadn't even had sex yet, for heaven's sake.

The thought was almost amusing—especially sitting here with her fiancé's brother, a guy she had actually slept with. Lost her virginity to, in fact. *Along with my heart.*

Was that why none of the others had stuck? She had wondered sometimes, usually late at night, if Zeke had broken something inside her. If, when he'd left, he'd taken something with him she could never get back. But now he was here and she'd decided she was better off without whatever it was he'd taken. Better off choosing a sensible, planned sort of relationship. Maybe it didn't burn with the same intensity, but she stood a better chance of making it out without injury.

She might not have been able to fulfil the role her father had hoped she would, after her mother's death. Maybe she hadn't been a great hostess or housekeeper, or able to help Helena in the way a mother would have. But those were never supposed to be her roles, anyway. Not in her father's household. This time she'd found her own role. Her own place in her own new family. And she wasn't giving that up.

She couldn't. Not when she risked returning to that empty, yawning loneliness that had followed Zeke's departure. With Zeke gone, Helena sent away for months, her father locked in his study and Isabella taking over everything Thea had thought was her responsibility…the isolation had been unbearable. As if the world had shifted in the wake of that horrible night and when it had settled there'd been no room for Thea any more. Nowhere she felt comfortable, at home.

And she'd been looking for it ever since. University hadn't provided it, and the holidays at home, with Helena floating around the huge house like a ghost, certainly hadn't. Working her way up at

Morrison-Ashton, proving she wasn't just there because of her father, that had helped. But a corner office wasn't a home, however hard she worked.

Flynn…their marriage, their family…he could be. And Thea couldn't let Zeke, or anyone, make her question that.

She watched Zeke, digging into his *pappardelle* and wondered why it was he'd really come back. Not for her—he'd made that much clear. So what was he trying to achieve?

'Zeke?'

He looked up from his bowl, eyes still unhappy. 'Yeah?'

'Why did you come back? Really? I mean, I know it wasn't just for my wedding. So why now?'

With a sigh, Zeke dropped his fork into his bowl and sat back. 'Because…because it was time. Because I'm done trying to win against my father. I'm done caring what he thinks or expects or wants. I'm ready to move on from everything that happened eight years ago.'

'Including me?'

'Including you.'

Thea took a breath, held it, and let it out. After this week they'd be done with each other for good.

She'd be married, and the past wouldn't matter any more. It felt…strange. Like an ache in a phantom limb. But she felt lighter, too, at the idea that everything could be put behind them at last.

Except, of course, she had one more thing to do before she could let him go.

Her gaze dropped down to her bowl as guilt pinged in her middle. This might be the one thing she could do to make sure Zeke never came back. But it was also one more step towards earning her place as an Ashton. And that meant it was worth it.

The way Thea's body relaxed visibly at his words left Zeke tenser than ever. Was she that relieved to be finally rid of even the memory of him? Or, like him, was she just so tired of lugging it all around every day? Was she happy to have the path clear for her happy-ever-after with Flynn? Or just settling for the safety of a sensible business marriage?

He'd ask…except those kind of questions—and caring about the answers—didn't exactly sound like leaving her behind.

One more day. He'd make sure she got down

the aisle, said 'I do', and rode off into the sunset. Then his new life, whatever it turned out to be, could begin.

'Before you leave us all behind completely, though...' Thea said.

Zeke's jaw clenched. There was always one more thing with Thea.

'I need to talk to you about something.'

A hollow opened up inside him. This was it. Whatever reason Thea had for dragging him out to buy a stupid gift for his brother, he was about to find it out. And suddenly he didn't want to know. If he had to leave her behind for ever he wanted to have this last day. Wanted to leave believing that she'd honestly wanted to spend time with him before he went. For the sake of everything they'd had once and knew they could never have again. Was that so much to ask?

Apparently so.

'I spoke to your father this morning,' Thea said, and Zeke's happy bubble of obliviousness popped.

'Did you, now?' He should have known that. Should have guessed, at least. He'd let himself get side-tracked by the experience of being with Thea again, and now he was about to get blindsided. Another reason why being around Thea Morrison was bad for his wellbeing.

'He wanted me to talk to you about—'

'About me selling This Minute to Morrison-Ashton,' Zeke finished for her. It wasn't as if his father had any other thoughts in relation to him.

'Yes.'

One simple word and the hollow inside him collapsed in on itself, like a punch to the gut folding him over.

'No,' he said, and let the anger start to fill him out again.

How could she ask? After everything they'd been to each other, everything they'd once had… how did she even dare?

His skin felt too hot and his head pounded with the betrayal. He knew exactly why she was doing it. To make sure he left. To make sure her perfect world went back to the way she thought it should be. To buy her place in his family, at his brother's side.

Because Morrison-Ashton and their families had always mattered more to her than he had. And he should have remembered that.

Thea pulled the face she'd always used to pull

when he'd been annoying her by being deliberately difficult. He'd missed that face until now. Now it just reminded him how little his feelings mattered to her.

'Zeke—'

'I'm not selling you my company, Thea.' He bit the words out, holding in the ones he really wanted to say. He wasn't that boy any more—the one who lost control from just being near her. This was business, not love. Not any more.

'Your father is willing to match whatever Glasshouse are offering...'

'I don't care.' *Just business*, he reminded himself.

'And even if you don't want to take up a position within Morrison-Ashton we could still look at share options.'

'I said no.' The rage built again, and he flexed his hand against his thigh to keep it from shaking.

'Our digital media team are putting together a—'

'Dammit, Thea!' Plates rattled as Zeke slammed his fist down on the table and the restaurant fell silent. 'Will you just listen to me for once?'

'Don't shout, Zeke,' Thea said, suddenly pale. 'People are looking.'

'Let them look.' He didn't care. Why should he? He'd be out of here tomorrow. 'Because I'm going to shout until you start listening to me.'

Thea's face turned stony. Dropping her fork into her bowl, she pulled out her purse and left several notes on the table. Then she stood, picked up her bag, and walked out of the restaurant.

The rage faded the moment she was out of his sight and he was Zeke Ashton the adult again. The man he'd worked so hard to become, only to lose him the moment she prodded at a sore spot.

Picking up his bottle of beer, Zeke considered his options. Then he drained the beer, dropped another couple of notes onto the stack and followed her, as he'd always known he would.

So had she known, it seemed, which irritated him more than it should have. Thea stood leaning against the wall of the restaurant, waiting for him.

'I left a very decent tip,' he said, watching her, waiting to see which way she'd jump. 'It seemed only fair since we walked out without finishing our meals.'

'Yelling suppresses the appetite.' Thea pushed away from the wall.

'It seemed the only way to get you to listen to me.'

Turning to face him, she smiled with obviously feigned interest. 'I'm listening.'

Suddenly his words felt petty, unnecessary. But he said them anyway. 'I will not sell This Minute to Morrison-Ashton.'

She gave a sharp nod. 'So you've mentioned. Now, if that's all, I want to go back to the villa.'

'What about Flynn's present?' Zeke asked, matching her stride as she headed for the car at speed.

'It can wait.'

'The wedding's tomorrow. I think you're pretty much out of time on this one.'

Thea opened the car door and slid into her seat. 'So I'll give him a spectacular honeymoon present instead.'

Zeke didn't want to think about what she might come up with for that. Except he already had a pretty good idea.

'Like the present you gave me for my twenty-first?' he asked, and watched Thea flush the same bright red as her car as she started the engine.

'You have to stop that,' she said, pulling away from the kerb.

'Stop what?' he asked, just to make her say it.

She glared at him. 'Look. I'm getting married tomorrow. So all this reminiscing about the good old days is getting kind of inappropriate, don't you think?'

'Oh, I don't know.' Zeke watched her as she drove, hands firm on the wheel, shoulders far more tense than they had been on the drive in. He was getting to her. And for some reason he really didn't want to stop. 'I think the question is whether Flynn thinks it's inappropriate.'

'Flynn doesn't know.'

'You mean you're not going to tell him about our shopping trip?'

'I mean he doesn't know about us at all. That we were ever…anything to each other.'

Thea took the last turning out of the town and suddenly their speed rocketed. Plastered back against his seat, Zeke tried to process the new reality she'd just confronted him with. She'd said they didn't talk about him, but he hadn't realised it extended this far. She'd written him out of their history completely, and the pain of that cut through his simmering anger for a moment.

'But…how?' How could anyone who knew them, who had seen them together back then, not known what they were to each other? They had been seventeen and twenty-one. *Subtle* hadn't really been in their vocabulary, despite Thea's requests to keep things secret. He hadn't cared who knew. Certainly their parents had known. How could Flynn have missed it?

'He was away at university, remember?' Thea said. 'And not just round the corner, like you. He was all the way up in Scotland. I guess he just… he was living his own life. I didn't realise at first, when we…started this. But it became clear pretty quickly. He just…didn't know.'

'And you didn't think it was important enough to tell him about?' Didn't think *he* was important enough. Suddenly Zeke wanted nothing more than to remind her just how important he'd been to her once.

'Why would I? You were gone. You were never coming back as far as I was concerned. And even if you did…even now you have…'

'Even now I have, what?'

'It doesn't change anything. You and I are ancient history, remember? What difference does it make now what we might have had eight years ago?'

But it did make a difference. Zeke couldn't say how, but it did. And suddenly he wanted her to admit that.

Thea tried to focus on the road, but her gaze kept slipping to the side, watching Zeke's reactions. It wasn't a test, wasn't as if she'd said anything untrue, but he wasn't reacting quite the way she'd expected.

She knew Zeke—had always known Zeke, it seemed. She knew that for him to come back now, into this situation…whatever his reasons… he wouldn't pass up the opportunity to drag up the past. He'd want his brother to feel uncomfortable, to know that he'd had her first. Punishment, she supposed. Partly for her, for not leaving with him, for breaking their deal. And partly for Flynn, for taking everything Zeke had always assumed was his.

Not telling Flynn… It had seemed like the best

idea at the time. And when Zeke had returned she'd been so relieved that she hadn't. One less thing to drive her crazy this week. Her relationship with Flynn might not be the most conventional, but their marriage agreement did have a fidelity clause, and she really didn't want to have an excruciatingly awkward conversation with her fiancé and probably their lawyers, maybe even their fathers, about whether Zeke's return would have any effect on that.

Of course it didn't. They'd both moved on. But Flynn liked to be thorough about these things.

'It makes a difference,' Zeke said suddenly, and Thea tried to tune herself back into the conversation, 'because you're lying to your fiancé. My brother.'

Thea gave a harsh laugh. 'Seriously? You're going to try and play the loving brother card? Now? It's a little late, Zeke.'

'I'm the best man at your wedding, Thea. Someone tomorrow is going to ask me if I know of any reason why you shouldn't get married.'

'You don't! Me sleeping with you eight years ago is not a reason for me not to get married tomorrow.'

Zeke raised an eyebrow. 'No? Then how about you lying to your fiancé? Or the fact you left your last two fiancés practically at the altar?'

'Why were you reading up on my love-life anyway?' She hadn't thought to ask when he mentioned Scott before. She'd been more concerned with getting the conversation away from her past romantic disasters. 'I don't believe for a second you just happened to stumble across that information on your site.'

'Did you think I hadn't kept up with you? Kept track of what was going on in your life?'

'Yes,' Thea said. 'That's exactly what I thought. I thought you left and forgot all about the people you left behind.'

'I didn't leave you behind.'

The countryside sped past faster than ever, but Thea couldn't bring herself to slow down. 'Zeke, you left and you didn't look back.'

'I asked you to come with me.' His mulish expression told her that even eight years couldn't change the fact that she'd said no. Too late now, anyway.

'And I told you I couldn't.'

Zeke shook his head. 'Not couldn't. Wouldn't.'

'It was eight years ago, Zeke! Does it really matter which now?'

'Yes!'

'For the love of God, why?'

'Because I've spent eight years obsessing about it and I need closure now, dammit! Preferably before you marry my brother and send me away again.'

Thea's head buzzed with the enormity of the idea. Eight years of obsession, and now he wanted closure. Fine. She'd give him his closure.

Slamming on the brakes, Thea pulled over to the side of the road, half into a field of sunflowers, and stopped the engine. Opening the door, she stepped out onto the dusty verge at the edge of the road, waiting for Zeke to follow. He did, after a moment, walking slowly around to where she leant against the car. She waited until he stopped, his body next to hers against the warm metal.

'You want closure?' she said.

'Yes.'

He wasn't looking at her—was choosing to stare out at the bright flowers swaying in the breeze instead. Somehow that made it all a little easier.

'Fine. What do you need to know to move on?'

Now he turned, his smile too knowing. 'I need to know that *you've* moved on. That you're not still making the same bad choices you made then for the same bad reasons.'

'I made the right choice,' Thea said, quietly. 'I chose to stay for a reason.'

'For Helena. For your father.'

'Yes.'

'You were living your life for other people to avoid upsetting your family, just like you are now.'

'No. I'm living my life for me.' And making the right decisions for the future she wanted. She had to hang on to that.

'Really? Whose idea was it for you to marry Flynn?'

'What difference does it make? I'm the one who chose to do it.'

'It makes a difference,' Zeke pressed.

Did the man not know how to just let go of something? Just once in his intense life? Was it too much to ask?

'Fine. It was your father's idea,' Thea said, bracing herself for the inevitable smugness. Lord, Zeke did love being right.

'Of course it was.' But he didn't sound smug.

Didn't sound vindicated. If anything, he sounded a little sad.

Thea turned to look at him. 'Why did you ask if you already knew?'

'Because I need you to see it. I need you to see what you're doing.'

His words were intense, but his eyes were worse. They pressed her, demanded that she look the truth in the face, that she open herself up to every single possibility and weigh them all.

Thea looked away, letting her hair fall in front of her face. 'I know what I'm doing.'

Zeke shook his head. 'No, Thea. I don't think you do. So, tell me. Why did you stay when I left?'

'Why do you think? We were too young, Zeke. And besides, my family needed me. Helena needed me.' More than ever right then.

'Why?'

'Oh, I don't know, Zeke. Why do you think? Why would a motherless teenage girl *possibly* need her big sister around to look out for her?' That wasn't the whole reason, of course, but the rest of it was Helena's secret to tell.

'She had your father. And my mother.'

A bitter laugh bubbled up in her throat. 'As

much as she might pretend otherwise, your mother is not actually *our* mother.'

'Just as well, really,' Zeke said, his voice low, and she knew without asking that he wasn't thinking about her marrying Flynn. He was thinking about all the things they'd done in dark corners at parties, about his twenty-first birthday, about every single time his skin had been pressed against hers.

And, curse him, so was she.

'I had to stay, Zeke,' she said.

'Give me one true reason.'

Thea clenched her hand against her thigh. Did the man simply not listen? Or just not hear anything he didn't like? 'I've given you plenty.'

'Those weren't reasons—they were excuses.'

'Excuses? My family, my future—they're excuses?' Thea glared at him. 'Nice to know you hold my existence in such high esteem.'

'That's not what this is about.'

'Then what *is* it about, Zeke?' Thea asked, exasperated. 'If you don't believe me—fine. Tell me why *you* think I stayed.'

'Because you were scared,' he said, without missing a beat.

'Ha!'

'You stayed because other people told you it was the right thing to do. Because you knew it was what your father would want and you've always, *always* done what he wanted. Because you've never been able to say no to Helena ever since your mother died.' He took a breath. 'But mostly you stayed because you were too scared to trust your own desires. To trust what was between us. To trust *me.*'

The air whooshed out of Thea's lungs. 'That's what you believe?'

'That's what I know.'

When had he got so close? The warm metal of the car at her back had nothing on the heat of his body beside her.

'You're wrong,' she said, shifting slightly away from him.

He raised an eyebrow. 'Am I?' Angling his body towards her, Zeke placed one hand on her hip, bringing him closer than they'd been in eight long years. 'Prove it.'

'How?' Thea asked, mentally chastising her body for reacting to him. This was over!

'Tell me you don't still think about us. Miss us being together. Tell me you don't still want this.'

Thea started to shake her head, to try and deny it, but Zeke lowered his mouth to hers and suddenly all she could feel was the tide of relief swelling inside her. His kiss, still so familiar after so long, consumed her, and she wondered how she'd even pretended she didn't remember how it felt to be the centre of Zeke Ashton's world.

Except she wasn't any more. This wasn't about her—not really. This was Zeke proving a point, showing himself *and* her that he could still have her if he wanted. And he'd made it very clear that he didn't—not for anything more than showing his father and his brother who had the power here. She was just another way for him to get one over on the family business.

And she had a little bit more self-respect than that, thank you.

'Thea,' Zeke murmured between kisses, his arm slipping further around her waist to haul her closer.

'No.' The word came out muffled against his mouth, so she put her hands against his chest and pushed. Hard.

Zeke stumbled back against the car, his hands abandoning her body to stop himself falling. 'What—?' He stopped, gave her one of those ironic, mocking looks she hated.

'I said no.' Thea sucked in a breath and lied. 'I *don't* still think about us. I *don't* miss what we had. It was a childish relationship that ran its course. I was ready for my own life, not just to hang on to the edges of yours. That's why I didn't come with you.' She swallowed. 'And I certainly don't want *that*. Especially not when I'm marrying your brother tomorrow.'

For once in his life Zeke was blessedly silent. Thea took advantage of the miracle by turning and getting back into the car. She focussed on her breathing…in and out, even and slow. Strapped herself in, started the engine. Familiar, easy, well-known actions.

And then she said, 'Goodbye, Zeke,' and gave him three seconds to clear the car before she screeched off back to the villa.

CHAPTER SEVEN

ZEKE STARED AFTER the cherry-red sports car kicking up dust as it sped away from him. Thea's dark hair blew behind her in the breeze, and he could still smell her shampoo, still feel her body in his arms.

He was an idiot. An idiot who was now stranded in the middle of nowhere.

Pushing his fingers through his hair, Zeke started the long trudge up the path towards the villa. At least Thea had driven him most of the way home before kicking him out.

Not that he could really blame her. He knew better than to ambush her like that. He'd just been so desperate to hear her admit it, to hear her say that she'd made a mistake not going with him that night.

That she still thought about him sometimes.

But clearly she didn't. She stood by her decision. And he had to live with that. At least for the next couple of days. Then he'd be gone, ready to start his own life for once, without the memories and the baggage of trying to prove his family wrong.

He'd told Thea he wanted closure, and she'd given it to him. In spades.

It was a long, hot, depressing walk back to the villa. By the time he got there, dusty and sweaty, the only thing he wanted in the world was a shower. It was nice, in a way, to have his desires pared down to the basics. Simpler, anyway.

Of course just because he only wanted one thing, it didn't mean he was going to get it. Really, he should have known that by now.

'Zeke!' Helena jumped up from her seat in the entrance hall, blonde waves bouncing. 'You're back! Great. I wanted to— What happened to you?'

'Your sister,' Zeke said, not slowing his stride as he headed straight for the stairs. 'She's trying to destroy my life, I think.'

'Oh,' Helena said, closer than he'd thought. Was she going to follow him all the way to his room?

'Don't worry,' Zeke told her. 'I know how to thwart her.' All he had to do was not sell his company to Morrison-Ashton—which he had no intention of doing regardless—and let her marry Flynn—which he appeared to have no choice in anyway.

Even if both things still made him want to punch some poor defenceless wall.

'Right…'

Helena sounded confused, but she was still following him. Clearly he needed to address whatever her problem was if he were to have any hope of getting his shower before the rehearsal dinner.

Sighing, Zeke stopped at the top of the stairs and leant against the cool, stone wall for a moment. 'You wanted to…?'

Helena blinked. 'Sorry?'

'You said you wanted to…'

'Talk to you!' Helena flashed him a smile. 'Yes. I did. I mean, I do.'

'Can it wait until after I've had a shower?'

She glanced down at the elegant gold watch on her slender wrist. 'Um…no. Not really.'

'Then I hope you can talk louder than the water pressure in this place.' Zeke pushed off the wall and continued towards his room. 'So, what's up, kid?'

'I'm hardly a kid any more, Zeke,' Helena said.

'I suppose not.' She had been when he'd left. Barely sixteen, and all big blue eyes and blonde curls. Actually, she was still the last two, but there was something in those big eyes. Little Helena had grown up, and he wondered how much he'd missed while he'd been gone. What had growing up in this family, this business, done to her? Because he already knew what it had done to Thea, and he wouldn't wish that on anyone.

'In fact I'm the maid of honour tomorrow. And you're the best man.'

Zeke froze outside his bedroom door. What on earth was she suggesting?

Helena's tinkling laugh echoed off the painted stone of the hallway. 'Zeke, you should see your face! Don't worry—I'm not propositioning you or anything.'

Letting his breath out slowly, so she wouldn't suspect he'd been holding it, Zeke turned the door handle. 'Never thought you were.'

'Yes, you did,' Helena said, brimming with confidence. It was nice to see, in a way. At least that hadn't been drummed out of her, the way it had Thea.

'So, what are you saying?' Zeke kicked his shoes

to the corner of the room, where they landed in a puff of road dust.

'We have responsibilities. We should co-ordinate them.' Letting the door swing shut behind her, Helena dropped down to sit on the edge of his bed, folding her legs up under her.

'As far as I can tell, other than an amusing yet inoffensive speech, I'm mostly superfluous to the proceedings.' Not that he cared. He knew his role here—show up and prove a point on behalf of the family that he was still a part of Morrison-Ashton. And he'd give them that for Flynn and Thea's wedding day. Not least because he knew it would be the last thing he ever had to give them. After tomorrow he'd be free.

'You're the best man, Zeke. It takes a little more than that.'

'Like dancing with you at the reception?' Stripping off his socks, Zeke padded barefoot into the bathroom to set the shower running. It took time to warm up, and maybe Helena would take the hint by the time it was at the right temperature.

'Like making sure the groom shows up.'

Zeke stopped. 'Why wouldn't he?' Did Helena know something he didn't? That *Thea* didn't?

'Because… Well…' Helena gave a dramatic sigh and fell back to lean against the headboard. 'Oh, I don't know. Because this isn't exactly a normal wedding, is it?'

That's what he'd been saying. Not that anyone—or at least not Thea—was listening. 'I'm given to understand that this is something they both want,' he said, as neutrally as he could.

Helena gave him a lopsided smile. 'She's been giving you the same line, huh? I thought maybe she'd admit the truth to *you*, at least.'

'The truth?' Zeke asked, when really what he wanted to say was, *Why me, 'at least'?*

'I know she thinks this is what she should do,' Helena said slowly. 'That it's the right thing for the company and our families. She wouldn't want to let anyone down—least of all Isabella or Dad.'

'But…?'

Tipping her head back against the headboard, Helena was silent for a long moment. Then she said, 'But…I think she's hoping this wedding will give her something it can't. And I don't think it's the right thing for her, even if she won't admit it.'

A warm burst of vindication bloomed in Zeke's

chest. It wasn't just him. Her own sister, the one she'd stayed for eight years ago, could see the mistake Thea was making. But his triumph was short-lived. There was still nothing he could do to change her decision.

Zeke sank down onto the edge of the bed. 'If you want to ask me to talk to her about it…you're about two hours too late. And, as you can see, it didn't go particularly well.' He waved a hand up and down to indicate the state of him after his long, hot, cross walk home.

Helena winced. 'What did she do? Leave you on the side of the road somewhere?'

'Pretty much.'

'Dammit. I really thought…'

'What?' Suddenly, and maybe for the first time ever, he really wanted to know what Helena thought. Just in case there was a sliver of a chance of it making a difference to how tomorrow went.

Helena gave a little one-shouldered shrug. 'I don't know. I guess I thought that maybe she'd talk to you. Open up. There was always something between you two, wasn't there? I mean, she never talked about it, but it was kind of obvious. So I thought…well, I hoped… But she's so scared of giving Dad and Isabella something else to use against her, to push her out...'

'That's what I told her,' Zeke said, but then something in Helena's words registered. 'What do you mean, push her out? And what was the first thing they used against her?'

She stared at him as if it wasn't possible he didn't already know. But then she blinked. 'Of course,' she murmured. 'It was the night you left. I told her...I told her right before her eighteenth birthday party—talk about insensitive. But I guess she never told you...'

Zeke was losing patience now. He felt as if there was a bell clanging in his head, telling him to pay attention, that this was important, but Helena kept prattling on and he *needed to know*.

'What, Helena? What did you tell her?' And, for the love of God, could this finally be the explanation he'd waited eight years for, only to have Thea deny him?

Helena gave him a long look. 'I'll tell you,' she said, her tongue darting out to moisten her lips. 'But it's kind of a long story. A long, painful story. So you go and have that shower, and I'll go and fetch some wine to make it slightly more bearable. I'll meet you back here in a little bit, yeah?'

Zeke wanted to argue—wanted to demand that she just *tell* him, already—but Helena had already slipped off the bed towards the door, and it looked as if once again he wasn't being given an option by a Morrison woman.

'Fine,' he said with a sigh, and headed for the shower.

At least he wouldn't stink of sweat and sun and roads when he finally got his closure.

She had her wedding rehearsal dinner in two hours. She should be soaking in the bath with a glass of something bubbly, mentally preparing herself for the next thirty-six hours or so. She needed to touch up a chip in her manicure, straighten her hair, check that her dress for the evening had been pressed. There were wedding presents to open, lists of thank-you notes to make, a fiancé to check in with, since she hadn't seen him all day... And at some point she should probably check with Housekeeping that Zeke had made it home alive—if only so she could slap him again later, or something.

But Thea wasn't doing any of those things. Instead she sat in Ezekiel Ashton's office, waiting for him to get off the phone with London. Just as she had been for the last forty minutes.

'Well, that's one way of looking at it, I suppose,' Ezekiel said into the receiver, and Thea barely contained her frustrated sigh.

Dragging a folder out of her bag she flipped through the contents, wishing she could pretend even to herself that they were in any way urgent or important. At least then she wouldn't feel as if she was wasting her time so utterly.

'The thing is, Quentin...'

Thea closed the folder. He could have asked her to come back later. He could have cut short his call. He could have looked in some way apologetic. But all Ezekiel had done was wave her into the visitor's chair and cover the receiver long enough to tell her he'd be with her shortly. Which had been a blatant lie.

She'd leave, just to prove a point, except he was almost her father-in-law and he already wasn't going to like the news she was bringing.

She sighed again, not bothering to hide it this time, and realised she was tapping her pen against the side of the folder. Glancing up at the desk, she saw Ezekiel raising his eyebrows at her.

Oops. Busted.

'I think I'm going to have to get back to you on that, Quentin,' he said, in his usual calm, smooth voice. The one that let everyone else know that as far as he was concerned he was the only person in the room that mattered. Zeke had always called it his father's 'Zeus the All-Powerful' voice. 'It seems that something urgent has come up at this end.'

Like the existence of his PR Director and soon-to-be daughter-in-law. Or perhaps the possibility of buying This Minute. Thea didn't kid herself about which of those was more important to the man across the desk.

'So, Thea.' Ezekiel hung up the phone. It was a proper old-fashioned one, with a handset attached by a cord and everything. 'Dare I hope that you're here with good news about my youngest son?'

Thea winced. 'Not...exactly.'

'Ah.' Leaning back in his seat, the old man steepled his fingers over his chest. 'So Zeke is still refusing to consider selling This Minute to Morrison Ashton?'

'I'm afraid so,' Thea said. 'He…he seems quite set on his decision, I'm afraid. And he says he's ready to move on from This Minute, so even offering him positions within the company didn't seem to help. He's looking for a new challenge.'

Ezekiel shook his head. 'That boy is always looking for an impossible challenge.'

He was wrong, Thea thought. Apart from anything else, Zeke was certainly no longer a boy. He'd grown up, and even if he'd always be twenty-one and reckless in the eyes of his family, *she* could see it. Had felt it in the way he'd kissed her, held her. Had known it when he'd told her the real reasons she hadn't left with him. He saw the truth even if she didn't want to face it. She *had* been scared. Even if in the end the choice had been taken away from her, and she'd had to stay for Helena, she knew deep down she'd never really thought she'd go. Hadn't been able to imagine a future in which she climbed out of that window and followed him.

Which was strange, because it was growing easier by the hour for her to imagine running out on this wedding and chasing after him. Not that she would, of course.

And not that he'd asked.

He'd wanted her to admit her mistake, had wanted to prove a point. But, kiss aside, there'd been no real thought or mention of wanting *her*.

Maybe Ezekiel was right. Maybe she was just his latest impossible challenge.

'Well, I can't say I'm not disappointed,' Ezekiel said, straightening in his chair. 'Still, I'm glad that you tried to convince him. That tells me a lot.'

Thea blinked at him. 'Tells you what, exactly?'

'It speaks to your commitment to the company—and to Flynn, of course. And it tells me that both you and Zeke have moved past your... youthful indiscretion.'

Heat flared in Thea's cheeks at his words. *Youthful indiscretion.* As if her history with Zeke was something to be swept under the carpet and forgotten about.

But wasn't that what she was doing by not telling Flynn about it?

Thea shook her head. 'I don't think that the childhood friendship Zeke and I shared would influence either of us in the matter of a business decision,' she said, as calmly and flatly as she could manage.

'Thea,' Ezekiel said, his tone mildly chastising. 'My son was in love with you once. He would have done anything for you. That he's said no to you on this matter tells me that he has moved on, that he no longer feels that way about you. And the fact that you asked him in the first place, knowing his...*feelings* for the family business— well, as I say, it's good to know where your loyalties lie.'

Nausea crept up Thea's throat as she listened to the old man talk. She knew he was right. She chosen work and business over a man she'd once thought hung the moon. Over someone who, whatever she might say to his face, still *mattered* to her. All because the old man across the desk had asked her to.

Worst of all was the sudden and certain knowledge that he'd known exactly what he was doing. This was the only reason Ezekiel had asked her to talk to Zeke about This Minute in the first place. It had been a test. Just like suggesting that she marry Flynn. Just like Zeke asking her for one true reason why she'd stayed. Just like her father, eight years ago, when she'd broken the news to him about Helena. Just like her first two engagements.

It was all a test—a way to find out if she was worthy of being a Morrison or an Ashton. Pushing her and prodding her to see how she'd react, how she'd cope, what decision she'd make, how she'd mess up this time. Her whole life was nothing more than a series of tests.

And the worst thing was she knew she was only ever one wrong answer away from failing. Just as she'd failed Helena.

Slowly, her head still spinning with angry thoughts, Thea got to her feet. 'I'm glad that you're satisfied, sir,' she said. 'Now, if you'll excuse me, I need to go and prepare for the rehearsal dinner.'

'Of course...of course.' Ezekiel waved a hand towards the door. 'After all, your most important role in this company is still to come tomorrow, isn't it?'

Thea barely managed a stiff nod before walking too fast out of the office, racing up the stairs, and throwing up in her bathroom.

When Zeke stepped out of the bathroom, a towel tightly tied around his waist, Helena was already sitting on his bed, halfway through a large glass of wine.

'Hang on.' Grabbing his suit hanger from the front of the wardrobe, he stepped back into the steam-filled bathroom and dressed quickly. At least he'd be ready for the rehearsal dinner early, and he'd feel better having whatever conversation this was fully dressed.

Helena handed him a glass of wine and he sat on the desk chair across the room, watching her, waiting for her to start.

She bit her lip, took another sip of wine, then said, 'Okay, so this isn't a story many people know.'

'Okay…'

'But I think it's important that you know it. It… Well, it might explain a bit about how Thea be-came…Thea.'

Anything that did that—that could explain how the free and loving girl he'd known had become the woman who'd left him at the side of the road today—had to be some story. 'So tell it.'

Helena's whole upper body rose and fell as she sucked in a breath. 'Right. So, it was a month or so before Thea's birthday. Before you left. I was sixteen. And stupid. That part's quite important.' She dipped her head, gazing down at her hands. 'Thea was babysitting for me one night. Dad was off at some business dinner, I guess. And even though I'd told him a million times that sixteen-year-olds don't need babysitters he was very clear. Thea was in charge. What she said went, and she was responsible for anything that happened while he was out.'

'Sounds like your dad,' Zeke murmured, wondering where this was going. 'I guess something happened that night?'

'I…I wanted to go out. I asked Thea, and she said no, so I nagged and whined until she gave in. I had a date with this guy a couple of years ahead of me in school. I knew Thea didn't like him, so I kinda left that part out when I told her I was going.'

Zeke had a very bad feeling about this story all of a sudden. 'What happened?' he asked, the words coming out raw and hoarse.

'He took me to his friend's house. There was beer, and some other stuff. And the next thing I knew…' Helena scrubbed a hand across her eyes. 'Anyway… They told me it was my own fault—

that I'd said yes and I just couldn't remember. I was so ashamed that I didn't tell anyone. Not even Thea. Not until six weeks later.'

'The night of her party?' Zeke guessed. She'd been crying, he remembered, when he'd climbed in her window to tell her he was going and ask if she'd decided to come or not. He'd thought it had been because she'd decided to stay.

'Yeah. I wouldn't have, but…I was pregnant.'

The air rushed out of Zeke's lungs. 'Oh, Helena…'

'I know. So I told Thea, and she told Dad for me, and then I got sent away for the summer until the baby was born.'

Helena's voice broke at last. Zeke thought most people would have given in to tears long before. Happy-go-lucky Helena hid a core of steel.

'She was adopted, and I never saw her again.'

Zeke crossed the room in a second, wrapping an arm around her as she cried. 'I should have been here.' Helena had been a little sister to him in a way Thea never had been. They'd been more. But Helena… Helena had been important to him too, and he hadn't even said goodbye. Hadn't dreamt of what she might be going through.

Helena gave a watery chuckle. 'What could you have done? Besides, I had Thea.'

This was what she'd meant. Why she'd had to stay. He'd always thought—believed deep down—that her words about Helena and her family were excuses. But they weren't. Helena really *had* needed her. Of course she'd stayed. But why hadn't she told him?

'But there's a reason I've told you this,' Helena said, snapping him back to the present. 'You have to understand, Zeke. Things changed after that night, and you weren't there to see it. You remember how it was—how Dad pushed her into taking over Mum's role after she died? He expected her to be able to do everything. School, the house, playing hostess for his clients, looking after me...'

'I remember,' Zeke said, bitterness leaking into his voice. She'd hated it so much. 'It was wrong. Hell, she was—what? Fourteen? Nobody should have that kind of responsibility at that age.'

'Well, she thought it *was* her responsibility. And so did he. So when all this happened...' Helena swallowed so hard Zeke could see it. 'He blamed her. Said that if she'd paid more attention it never would have happened. He took it all away from her. And that was when Isabella stepped in.'

'My mum?'

Helena nodded. 'She took over. She ran our house as well as yours. She became part of the family more than ever. She looked after me, played hostess for Dad...'

'She pushed Thea out,' Zeke finished for her. How had he not noticed that? Not noticed how little a place Thea seemed to have, even in her own wedding.

'Yeah. I wasn't here to start with, so I don't really know the whole of it. But ever since it's been like Thea's been trying to find her way back in. Find a place where she belongs.'

'And you think that's why she's marrying Flynn?'

Helena tilted her head to the side. 'I don't know. That's what I... I worry, that's all.'

And she was right to. Of *course* that was what Thea was doing. She'd practically admitted as much to him, even if he hadn't understood her reasoning.

'And the thing is, Zeke,' Helena went on, 'despite everything Thea blames herself for what happened to me and what happened next. She always has. Even though it isn't her fault—of course it isn't. But she was responsible for me that night. That's what Dad told her. And she thinks that if she hadn't let me go out that night everything would have been different.'

'*Her* fault?' Zeke echoed, baffled. 'How can she possibly…?'

'She calls it the biggest mistake she ever made.'

Suddenly Zeke was glad that Helena didn't know what Thea had given up to stay with her. He couldn't blame either of them any more. But could he make Thea see that one mistake didn't mean she had to keep making the same safe decisions her whole life?

'Thank you for telling me this, Helena.'

Helena gave a little shrug. 'Did it help?'

'Yeah. I think so.'

Pulling away, Helena watched his face as she asked, 'So, do you think you can talk Thea out of this wedding?'

'I thought I was supposed to be making sure the groom showed up on time?'

'If she decides to go through with it, yeah. But I want to be very sure that she's doing this for the right reasons. Not just because she's scared of being pushed out again for not doing what the family wants.'

Zeke grinned. 'Looks like we're on the same side, then.'

'Good.' Standing up, Helena smoothed down her dress and wiped her eyes. 'About time I had some help around here. Now, come on, best man. We've got a rehearsal dinner to get to.'

'And a wedding to get called off,' Zeke agreed, following her to the door.

He had his closure now, but he had far more, too. He had the truth. The whole story. And that was what would make all the difference when he confronted Thea this time.

CHAPTER EIGHT

THEA SCANNED THE dining room through the crack of the door, then glanced down at her deep red sheath dress, wondering why she felt as if she was walking into a business dinner. Of all the people she'd recognised in the room, waiting for them to walk in, only three had been family. Everyone else was someone she'd met across a conference table. This time tomorrow she'd be married, and her whole new life would start. But she was very afraid, all of a sudden, that her new life might be a little too much like her old one.

'Ready?' Flynn asked, offering her his arm.

He looked handsome in his suit, Thea thought. All clean-shaven and broad shoulders. Safe. Reliable. Predictable. Exactly what she'd decided she wanted in life.

'Or do you want to sneak into Dad's study for a shot of the good brandy before we face the gathered hordes?'

Thea smiled. 'Tempting, but probably not advisable. Besides, your Dad's almost certainly still working in there.'

'There is that.' Flynn sighed. 'I had hoped he'd see this as more of a family celebration than a networking opportunity.'

Nice to know she wasn't the only one who had noticed that. 'I guess he doesn't see any reason why it can't be both. I mean, he knows our reasons for getting married. He helped put together the contract, for heaven's sake.'

'Yeah, I know,' Flynn said, sounding wistful. 'It's business. I just… It would be nice if we could pretend, just for a couple of days, that there's something that matters more to us.'

Thea stared at him. She was going to marry this man tomorrow, and she'd never once heard him speak so honestly about their life or their relationship.

'Flynn? Are you…?' *Are you what? Getting cold feet? Unhappy with me? Not the time for that conversation, Thea.* 'Did you want to wait? To get married, I mean? To someone you're actually in love with?'

Because it was one thing to marry a man you

didn't love because that was the deal. Another to do it when he was secretly holding out for more. She thought back to their conversation on the porch, about kids and the future. How happy he'd been at the idea of a family.

But Flynn shook his head, giving her a self-deprecating smile. 'Don't listen to me,' he said. 'We're doing the right thing here. For us and for the business. And, yeah, the fairytale would be nice, I guess. But it's not all there is. And who knows? Maybe you and I will fall in love one day.'

But they wouldn't, Thea knew, with the kind of sudden, shocking certainty that couldn't be shifted. As much as she liked, respected and was fond of Flynn, and as much as she enjoyed his company, she wasn't ever going to be in love with him. She knew how that felt, and it wasn't anything like this.

Thea tried to smile back, but it felt forced. 'Are you ready to go in?' she asked, wishing she'd just said yes when he'd asked her the same question. The knowledge she'd gained in the last two minutes seemed too much for her body—as if she could barely keep it inside on top of every other thought she'd had and fact she'd learned since Zeke came home.

'As I'll ever be,' Flynn said, flashing her a smile. 'Let's go.'

He pushed the door open and the volume level of conversation in the room dipped, then dropped, then stalled. Everyone stood, beaming at them, waiting for them to walk in and take their seats as if they were some kind of royalty. And all Thea could see was Zeke and Helena, standing together near the head of the huge table, leaning into each other. Helena murmured something Thea couldn't hear, and Zeke's lips quirked up in a mocking grin. Talking about her? Thea didn't care. All she knew was that she wanted to be over there, chatting with them, and not welcoming the fifty-odd other people who had somehow got themselves invited to her rehearsal dinner.

She let Flynn take the lead. His easy way with people meant that all she had to do was smile and nod, shake the occasional hand. She let him lead her to their seats, smiled sweetly at everyone around them as she sat down.

Her father nodded to Flynn, and Isabella said,

'Oh, Thea, you look so beautiful tonight. And those pearls are a perfect match! I'm so glad.'

Thea's hand unconsciously went to the necklace Isabella had given her. The perfectly round pearls were hard and cold under her fingers. You were supposed to wear pearls often, weren't you? To keep them warm and stop them cracking or drying, perhaps?

'Aren't pearls supposed to be bad luck?' Helena asked, topping up her glass of wine from the bottle on the table.

'Oh, I don't think so,' Isabella said, laughing lightly. 'And, besides, who believes those old superstitions, anyway?'

'"Pearls mean tears",' Helena quoted, her voice firm and certain. 'And you're the one who insisted on Thea having all the old, new, borrowed and blue stuff.'

'I like pearls,' Thea said, glancing in surprise at her sister. It wasn't like Helena to antagonise Isabella. For a moment it was almost as if the old teenage Helena was sitting beside her. 'I don't think they mean anything.'

There was silence for a moment, before the doors opened and a fleet of waiters entered, ready to serve the starters. They waited until every bowl was ready and in position, then lowered them all to the table at the same time, before disappearing again as silently as they'd come.

'Saved by the soup,' Zeke murmured from two seats down as he reached for the butter.

Thea studied him as he buttered his roll, and kept watching as Helena topped up his wine, too. He must have walked home, she supposed. His forehead was ever so slightly pink from the sun. But he didn't seem angry, or tense as he had earlier. He seemed calm, relaxed. Even happy.

Maybe he'd got the closure he needed. Maybe he was thinking ahead to leaving the day after tomorrow. To selling This Minute to Glasshouse and moving on to his new life. Thea could see how that might be appealing. Not that she had that option. She didn't want out of this family—she wanted in.

Besides, Zeke had been gone eight years already and still not really moved on. What reason was there to believe he'd be able to put it all behind him for real this time?

Isabella and Flynn kept up the small talk across the table through all three courses. Thea drank her wine too quickly and tried to pretend her head wasn't spinning. And then, as the waiters came round to pour the coffee, her father stood up and clinked his fork against his glass.

'Oh, no,' Thea whispered. 'What's he doing?'

Flynn patted her hand reassuringly, somehow managing to make her even more nervous.

'I know tonight isn't the night for big speeches,' Thomas Morrison said. 'And, trust me, I'll have the traditional light, adoring and entertaining father of the bride speech for you all tomorrow. But I wanted to say a few words tonight for those of you who've been so close to our family all these years. Who've seen us through our dark times as well as our triumphs.'

'Which explains why almost everyone here is a business associate,' Helena muttered, leaning across towards Thea. 'We've barely seen any family since Mum died.'

'Shh…' Isabella said, without moving her lips or letting her attentive smile slip.

'You all know that getting here, to this happy event, hasn't always been a smooth path. And let me say candidly that I am both delighted and relieved that Thea has finally made a decision in her personal life that's as good as the ones she makes at work!'

The laughter that followed buzzed in Thea's ears, but she barely heard it. Her body felt frozen, stiff and cold and brittle. And she knew, suddenly, that even marrying Flynn wouldn't be enough. To her father she'd still always be a liability. A mistake just waiting to happen.

'And I want to say thank you to the person who has made all this possible,' Thomas went on, waving his arm expansively to include the food, the villa, and presumably, the wedding itself.

Thea held her breath, bracing herself for the blow she instinctively knew was coming next.

'My dear, dear friend, Isabella Ashton.'

More applause—the reverent sort this time. People were nodding their heads along with her father's words, and Isabella was blushing prettily, her smile polite but pleased.

Thea thought she might actually be sick.

'So, let us all raise our glasses to the mother of the groom and the woman who has been as a mother to the bride for the last twelve years.'

Chairs were scraped back as people stood, and the sound grated in her ears. Wasn't it enough that she'd given them all what they wanted? She was marrying the families together, securing their future, their lineage, and the future of their business. And even today, the night before her wedding, she wasn't worthy of her father's approval, or love.

Thea staggered to her feet, clutching the edge of the table, as the guests lifted their glasses and chanted, 'Isabella!' Even Flynn, next to her, had his wine in the air and was smiling at his mother, utterly unaware of how his fiancée's heart had just been slashed with glass.

It was almost as if she wasn't there at all.

Zeke watched Thea's face grow paler as Thomas wound up his ridiculous speech. Who said something like that about his own daughter the day before her wedding? Especially when that daughter was Thea. He *had* to know how sensitive she was about her perceived mistakes, surely? And then to toast Isabella instead… That had been just cruel and callous.

Maybe he truly didn't care. Not if he could get in a good joke, amuse his business associates… Zeke ground his teeth as he waited for his coffee to cool. He'd never been Thomas Morrison's biggest fan, but right then he loathed the man more than he'd ever thought possible.

Thomas sat down to a round of applause and more laughter, and Zeke saw Thea visibly flinch. Flynn, however, was shaking his father-in-law-to-be's hand and smiling as if nothing had happened. As if he couldn't see how miserable Thea was. He was going to marry her tomorrow and he couldn't even see when her heart was breaking.

Zeke gulped down his rage at his brother along with his coffee. All that mattered was getting Thea the hell out of there.

Helena appeared over his left shoulder suddenly, pushing something cold and bottle-shaped into his hand. 'Go on,' she said, nodding towards Thea. 'I'll cover for you both here.'

'Thanks,' Zeke murmured, keeping the bottle of champagne below table level as he stood. Catching Thea's eye, he raised his eyebrows and headed for the door, not waiting to see if she followed. Helena would make sure that she did.

Outside on the terrace the air held just a little bite—a contrast to the blazing sun he'd walked back in earlier. Dropping onto the swing seat, Zeke held up the bottle and read the label. The good stuff, of course. Old Thomas wouldn't serve anything less while he was insulting his daughter in front of everyone she'd ever met. Shame Helena hadn't thought to provide glasses… Although, actually, swigging expensive champagne from the bottle with Thea brought back its own collection of memories.

The door to the hallway opened and Thea appeared, her face too pale against her dark hair and blood-red dress. Her skin seemed almost translucent in the moonlight, and suddenly Zeke wanted to touch it so badly he ached.

'Have a seat,' he said, waving the bottle over the empty cushion beside him. 'I think your sister thought you might need this.'

'She was right.' Thea dropped onto the seat next to him, sending the whole frame swinging back and forth. 'Although why she decided I also needed you is beyond me.'

'Ouch.' Unwrapping the wire holding it in place, Zeke eased the cork out of the neck of the bottle. He didn't want the pop, the fizz, the explosion. Just the quiet opening and sharing of champagne with Thea. To show her that *he* knew tonight was about her, even if no one else seemed to.

'Oh, you know what I mean,' Thea said, reaching over to take the bottle from him. 'We're not having the best day, apart from anything else.'

'I don't know what you're complaining about,' Zeke said. 'You weren't the one left in the middle of nowhere in the blazing heat.'

Thea winced, and handed him the bottle back. 'Sorry about that.'

'No, you're not.' Zeke lifted the bottle to his mouth and took a long, sweet drink. The bubbles popped against his throat and he started to relax for the first time that day.

'Well, maybe just a little bit. You deserved it, though.'

'For telling the truth?'

'For kissing me.'

'Ah. That.'

'Yeah, *that.*'

Zeke passed the bottle back and they sat in silence for a long moment, the only sound the occasional wave of laughter from inside or the squeaking of the hinges on the swing.

'I'm not actually all that sorry about that, either,' Zeke said finally.

Thea sighed. 'Yeah. Me neither. Maybe we

needed it. You know—for closure, or whatever you were going on about.'

'Actually, your sister helped me with that more than you did.'

Thea swung round to stare at him, eyes wide. 'Tell me you have *not* been kissing my sister this afternoon.'

'Or what?'

'Or I'll drink the rest of this champagne myself.' She took a long swig to prove her point.

Zeke laughed. 'Okay, fine. I have not been kissing Helena. This afternoon or any other.'

'Good.'

'Not that it would be any of your business if I had.'

'She's my sister,' Thea said, handing back the champagne at last. 'She'll always be my business.'

'But not your responsibility,' Zeke said. 'She's an adult now, Thea. She can take care of herself.'

'Perhaps.' Thea studied him carefully. 'When you said that Helena had helped you find closure…what did you mean?'

Zeke tipped his head back against the swing cushion. 'She told me some of what happened. Things I didn't know. About what really happened the night of your eighteenth birthday. Why you didn't come with me. And about what happened next.'

He heard the breath leave Thea's lungs in a rush. 'She told you? About the…?'

'About what happened to her. And about the baby.' He rolled his head to the left to watch her as he added, 'And how it really wasn't your fault.'

Thea looked away. 'That's up for debate.'

'No. It isn't.' No response. 'Thea. Look at me.' She didn't. 'Why?'

'Because I'm about to say something that matters and I want to be sure that you're listening to me.'

Slowly she lifted her head and her gaze met his. Zeke felt it like a jolt to the heart—the connection he'd thought they'd lost was suddenly *right there.* Part of him again after all these years.

'Whatever mistakes you think you've made in your life, Thea, that wasn't one of them. You cannot make yourself responsible for what those boys did to her.'

'My father did,' Thea whispered. 'I was in charge. I was responsible. And I let her go out.'

'No.' He had to make her understand. Wrapping his arm around her shoulder, he pulled her closer, still keeping them face to face, until she was pressed up against his chest. 'Listen to me, Thea. It wasn't your fault. And you can't live your whole life as if it was.'

Thea stared up into his eyes for a long moment. They were filled with such sincerity, such certainty. Why could she never feel that way about her life? That unshakeable conviction that whatever choice she made was the right one. That fearlessness in the face of mistakes.

Of course in Zeke it also led to occasional unbearable smugness, so maybe she was better off without.

Swallowing, Thea pulled away, and Zeke let her go. 'Is that what you think I'm doing?'

'I know it,' Zeke said, unbearable smugness firmly in place.

'You're wrong, you know,' she said conversationally, looking down at her hands.

Part of her still couldn't believe that Helena had really told him everything. She'd barely discussed it with Thea ever since it happened. As far as she knew Helena had never willingly told anyone else about it—something their father and Isabella had been in full support of. After all, why make a scandal when you can hide one? And coming so soon after Zeke running away... Well, no one wanted to make headlines again. Thea assumed that Ezekiel Senior knew, but maybe not. Isabella had taken care of everything. Maybe she'd never seen the need to brief him on the shocking events.

'Am I? As far as I can see you stayed eight years ago for Helena, and because you were scared. And now—'

'I made the right decision eight years ago,' Thea interrupted. Because if he had to know everything at least he could admit that much. 'And I don't regret it for a moment.'

'Fair enough,' Zeke said, more amicably than she'd expected. 'And we'll never know how things might have worked out if Helena hadn't gone out that night, or if she'd waited one more day to tell you about it. But the point is Helena's all grown up now. She doesn't need you to protect her any more. And yet you're still staying.'

She shook her head. 'My whole life is here. My place is here.'

'Is it?' He gripped her arm, tightly enough that she had to pay attention. 'They pushed you out, Thea.'

The coldness that settled over her was familiar. The same chill she'd felt that whole summer after Zeke had left. 'You don't…you don't know what it was like.'

'Helena told me. She told me everything.'

But that wasn't enough. A description, a few words—it couldn't explain how it felt to have your whole existence peeled away from you. She wasn't sure if even she could explain it to him. But she knew she had to try…had to make him understand somehow.

'It was as if I'd stopped even existing,' she whispered in the end. 'I couldn't be what Dad needed, so there was no place for me any more. I wasn't good enough for him.'

Zeke's grip loosened, but just enough to pull her against his body. She could feel his heart, thumping away in his chest, and the memory of how his arms had always felt like home cut deeper now.

'Then why are you trying so hard to get back

in? Surely you can see you're better off without him. Without all of them.'

'You think I should run away, like you?' She pulled back enough to give him a half-smile. 'This is my place. Besides, where else would I go, Zeke?'

'Anywhere! Anywhere you can be yourself. Live your own life. Not make decisions about your personal happiness based on what is best for the family business, or what our fathers want you to do. Anywhere in the world, Thea.' He paused, just for a moment, then added, 'You could even come with me, if you wanted.'

Thea's heart stopped dead in her chest. She couldn't breathe. She couldn't think. Couldn't process what he was saying…

'I'm marrying Flynn tomorrow.' The words came out without her permission, and she watched Zeke's eyes turn hard as she spoke.

'Why?' he asked. 'Seriously, Thea. Tell me why. I don't understand.'

'I love him.'

'No, you don't.'

'I might!'

Zeke laughed, but there was no humour in the

sound. 'Thea, I'm sure you do love him—in a way. But don't try and tell me you're in love with him, or vice versa. He didn't even notice how distressed you were tonight.'

'*You* did.' She could hear the anger in his voice as he talked about Flynn. Was that for her?

He gave a slight nod. 'Me and Helena. We're your team.'

'And you're leaving me tomorrow.' How could he offer her a place in the world when he didn't even know where he'd be tomorrow? Didn't he understand? She needed more than that. Somewhere she could never be pushed out or left behind. Somewhere she was enough.

'Yeah.'

'Great teamwork, there.'

Thea stared out into the darkness of the Tuscan hills beyond. She hadn't answered Zeke's question—something she knew he was bound to call her on before too long. But what could she say? Whatever it was, he wouldn't agree or approve. Should that matter? She didn't want Zeke to leave hating her. But why not? She would never see him again once she was married. He'd made that perfectly clear. If all she was protecting was the memory of something already eight years dead, what was the point?

'So?' Zeke asked eventually. 'The truth this time. Why are you so set on marrying Flynn tomorrow?'

'Maybe I think it'll make me happy,' Thea said.

Zeke shifted, turning his body in towards hers, one knee bent to let his leg rest on the seat. 'Do you? Think you'll be happy?'

She considered lying, but there didn't seem much point. Zeke never believed her anyway. 'I think I'll be safe. Secure. I'll have someone to help me make the right decisions. I think I'll have the agreement of all my friends and family that I'm not making a mistake.'

'Not all of them,' Zeke muttered.

'I think I'll have a place here again. A place I've earned…a place I belong. One that's mine by blood and marriage and can never be taken away from me. I'll be content,' Thea finished, ignoring him.

'Content? And is that enough for you?'

Thea shrugged. 'What else is there?' she asked, even though she knew the answer.

'Love. Passion. Happiness. Pleasure.'

'Yeah, you see, that's where I start to make mistakes. I know business. I know sensible, well thought out business plans. I know agreements, contracts, promised deliverables. Pleasure is an unknown quantity.'

Zeke shifted again and he was closer now, his breath warm against her cheek. Thea's skin tingled at the contact.

'You used to know about pleasure,' he said, his voice low.

'That was a long time ago,' Thea replied, the words coming out huskily.

'I remember, though. You used to crave pleasure. And the freedom to seek it. To do what felt right and good, not what someone said you were supposed to do.'

His words were hypnotising. Thea could feel her body swaying into his as he spoke, but she couldn't do anything to stop the motion. The swing beneath them rocked forwards and back, and with every movement she seemed to fall closer and closer into Zeke. As if gravity was drawing her in. As if nothing she could say or do or think could stop it.

'Don't you miss it?' he whispered, his mouth

so close to hers she could feel the words on her own lips.

'Yes,' she murmured, and he kissed her.

CHAPTER NINE

SHE TASTED JUST as Zeke remembered—as if it had been mere moments since his mouth had last touched hers. This wasn't the angry kiss of earlier that day, a kiss that had been more punishment than pleasure. This…this was something more.

Pleasure and pain mingled together. The years fell away and he was twenty-one again, kissing her goodbye even as he hoped against hope that she might leave with him.

Maybe this time it would end differently. Maybe this time he could persuade her. After all, he'd learnt a lot in eight years.

Slipping a hand around her back, he held her close, revelling in the feel of her body against his, back where she belonged. How had he let himself believe, even for a moment, that he could watch her marry someone else and then walk away?

Flynn… The thought of his brother stalled him for a moment, until he remembered him shaking

Thomas's hand after that godforsaken speech. He didn't know Thea—didn't know what she needed, let alone what she wanted. He didn't love her any more than Thea loved him. Zeke knew that for sure.

Maybe he'd even understand. And even if he didn't…Zeke was close to the edge of not caring. Flynn didn't deserve her—he'd proved that tonight. And Zeke needed this. Needed her more than ever before.

Zeke ran his palms up Thea's back, deepening the kiss, and felt his heartbeat quicken at the little noises she made. Half moans, half squeaks, they let him know exactly how much more she wanted. And how much he planned to give her…

'Zeke,' Thea murmured, pulling back just a little. 'What about—?'

'Shh…' Zeke trailed his fingers over her neck, feeling her shiver against him. 'Just pleasure, remember?'

Thea gave a little nod, as if she couldn't help but agree, and Zeke took that as permission to kiss her again. First her lips, deep and wanting. Then her jaw, her neck, her collarbone, down into the deep V of her dress and the lacy bra beyond.

'Oh, Zeke.' Thea shuddered again as his hand crept up her thigh, under her skirt, and he smiled against her skin. He remembered this, too. Remembered how natural it felt to have her in his arms, how she responded to his every touch, every kiss. How she arched up against him, her body begging for more. How could she pretend that she wanted anything other than this, than *him*, when her whole body told him otherwise?

He wanted to get her upstairs. Wanted her in his bed, her naked skin against his. But he knew that he had only this moment to convince her, to change her mind, and he couldn't risk the pause being enough to break her out of pleasure's spell. No, he knew Thea. With cold air between them, and a whole staircase to climb to find a bed, she'd start doubting herself. He didn't have time for her to have second thoughts. She was supposed to get married tomorrow, and he couldn't let that happen.

So it would have to be here. He'd seduce her right here on the terrace. Then she'd see she couldn't marry Flynn. And Flynn would understand that. Wouldn't he?

Tightening his hold on her, Zeke pulled Thea up

from the swing across onto his lap, so her knees fell neatly either side of his thighs, all without breaking their kiss. Her body seemed to know exactly what he had planned, moving with his without hesitation. As if it had done it before… Which, of course, it had. Zeke smiled at the memory.

'This remind you of anything?' he murmured, kissing his way back up her throat.

Thea murmured in agreement. 'Your twenty-first birthday party.'

'Out on the balcony…'

'With the party going on right underneath us.'

'That was all *you*, you know.'

Thea pressed against him and he couldn't help but gasp.

'I seem to remember you being there, too.'

'Yeah, but you're the one who dragged me up there.' He could see it now, in his memories. The bright blue dress she'd worn, the naughty look in her eye, the way she'd bitten her lip as she raised her eyebrows and waited for him to follow her into the house…

'I didn't hear you complaining,' Thea said, her hands pushing his shirt up to get to his skin.

Zeke sucked in a breath at the feel of her fingers on his chest. 'I really wasn't.'

She stilled for a moment, and Zeke's hands tightened instinctively on her thighs, keeping her close. 'What is it?' he asked.

'I just… I've never felt that again. What I felt that night, with you…'

The words were a whisper, an ashamed admission, but Zeke's eyelids fluttered closed in relief at the sound of them. 'Me neither. It's never been like it was with you. Not with anyone.' Never felt so much like coming home.

She kissed him then, her hands on his face, deep and loving, and he knew for the first time in eight years that things were going to be okay again.

'Make love to me, Zeke,' Thea whispered, and Zeke looked up into her eyes and smiled.

'Always.'

Thea blinked in the darkness and wondered how it was possible that she'd forgotten this feeling. The sense that her whole body had relaxed into the place where it belonged. That moment of sheer bliss and an empty mind.

Maybe she hadn't forgotten. Maybe, as great

as her memories were, it had never been like this for them before. Because, seriously, surely she'd remember something that good.

She breathed in one last breath of satisfaction… pleasure and *home.*

Then she sat up and faced the real world again.

Her senses and thoughts crashed in immediately—a whole parade of them, ranging from her complete idiocy to her goosebumps. It was cold on the terrace…colder than Thea had thought Tuscany could be in the summer. Of course it would probably be warmer if she was still wearing her dress… Beside her Zeke lay on the swing seat, his shirt unbuttoned to reveal a broad expanse of tanned chest.

Somehow this seemed far more dignified for men.

Reaching for her dress and slipping it over her shoulders, Thea tried to stop her mind spinning with the idea of what she'd just done. She'd cheated on her fiancé. She'd become *that* woman—the one who made a stupid mistake that might cost her everything. The night before her own wedding. At her rehearsal dinner! All because Zeke had started talking about pleasure and making her remember how good things had used to be... And hadn't she just finished telling him that wasn't what she wanted any more?

But she couldn't blame Zeke, however manipulated she felt. She'd wanted it. Asked for it, even. All he'd done was give her what she'd craved. What she'd spent eight years trying to forget.

Thea sighed and Zeke stirred at the sound, snaking an arm around her waist to pull her closer. She sank into him as if, having given in once, all her will power had gone.

This was the hardest part. If it was just great sex with Zeke she was giving up it would be easy. Well, maybe not easy, but certainly doable. But that wasn't all it was.

'You're thinking too loudly,' Zeke murmured against her ear, and she sighed again.

It wasn't the sex. It was the way her body felt in tune with his...the way he could anticipate what she needed before she knew she needed it. The way she felt right in his arms. The way she fitted—*they* fitted together. Not just physically, either.

It just felt so natural with Zeke, in a way she knew it never would with Flynn.

But was that enough?

Zeke might know what she needed, but there was no guarantee that he'd give it to her. As much as she'd loved him when they were younger, she knew him, too. Knew what mattered most to him. And while he might have proclaimed from the rafters that the only thing that mattered to him was her, in the end he'd still left her behind when she wouldn't fit in with his plans. Hadn't even listened when she'd tried to explain why she couldn't go.

Sometimes she wondered if it really had been love. It had felt like it, then. But they'd been kids. What had they known?

And even now Zeke didn't understand about doing the careful thing, the *right* thing. About not taking the risk of making things worse. For him, the risk was half the fun—always had been. He'd liked the thought of getting caught at his twenty-first birthday party. And she knew, from watching This Minute grow and develop through the business pages, that half the fun for Zeke was knowing that he was only ever one step, one chance, one risk away from it all coming down. He'd been lucky—brilliant too, of course—but it could have gone either way.

And Thea didn't have room for any more mistakes in her life. Couldn't risk being left with nothing, no place, again.

'Seriously,' Zeke said, shifting to sit up properly, his shirt flapping closed over his chest.

That might make it easier for her to think clearly, at least.

'What's going on in that head of yours?'

Thea sat up. 'I have to go. I need to… My guests are inside.'

Zeke's expression hardened. Reaching over, he picked up her bra and held it out to her, dangling from his fingers. 'You might need this.'

Thea snatched it from him. 'What did you think I was going to do next, Zeke? I'm supposed to be getting married tomorrow, and I'm out here with the best man! That's never a good decision.'

He shook his head ruefully. 'I should have known. You think I'm a mistake.'

'I didn't say that, Zeke.' She never would, knowing how much of his childhood he'd spent thinking that. That his parents would have been happier with just Flynn, their planned and chosen child, rather than the biological one who had come along at exactly the wrong moment. 'I just…I need to tell Flynn.' That much was a given, surely? 'I need to sort all this out.'

Zeke blew out a breath and settled back against the swing. 'Yeah, okay. I guess disappearing in the middle of the night at some party never was your style, was it?'

'No, that was all you.' Thea gave him a sad smile, remembering that night eight years ago and knowing with absolute certainty, for the first time, that she could never have gone with him even if Helena hadn't needed her. She wasn't built for Zeke's kind of life.

She just hoped he realised that, too.

Zeke watched Thea walk back inside, her hair no longer so groomed and her make-up long gone. Would she go and fix herself up first? What was the point, if she was just going to tell Flynn that she couldn't marry him? Sure, Flynn would know exactly what they'd been doing, but was that such a bad thing? It gave a point-of-no-return sort of feel to things.

Settling back against the swing seat, Zeke pushed aside the guilt that flooded him at the thought of his brother. It wasn't a love match; he knew that. And this wasn't like when they were kids. He wasn't taking Thea just so that Flynn couldn't have her. She belonged with him—always had. Surely Flynn would understand that?

He hoped so. With conscious effort Zeke relaxed his muscles, feeling the happy thrumming that buzzed through his blood, the reminder of everything the evening had brought him. Who would have thought, when she'd dumped him on the roadside that afternoon, that the day would end here?

He should have known that appealing to her reasonable side wouldn't work. Thea wasn't like other people. She needed to see the truth, *feel* it, not just be told it. Why hadn't he remembered that?

It didn't matter now. He'd shown her they belonged together. Even her most conservative, analytical, risk-averse side couldn't deny that now. She wanted a place to belong? He could give her that. He could give her everything she needed if she let him. Finally they'd get the life they'd been denied eight years ago, and he was going to make it so good for her. Make her loosen up a bit, reveal the Thea he knew was hiding in there somewhere.

Once the sale of This Minute went through to Glasshouse they could go anywhere, do anything. Maybe they'd just travel for a bit, see the world, get to know one another again as adults. He'd have to take things slowly, so as not to scare her. He knew Thea: even after the jump forward their relationship had taken this evening she was bound to scuttle a few paces back. But Zeke didn't care how slowly it went, how much he had to gentle her along. He'd have Thea in his arms every night, just as he'd always wanted. This time *he* was her choice. Not Flynn, not Helena, not the business, not her father or his. *Him*. Zeke. And he could live with everything in their past as long as he was her last choice.

Zeke smiled to himself as he listened to the sounds of the dinner finishing up and people starting to leave inside. He'd go back in soon, find Thea when she was ready for him.

Sure, there was a lot to figure out first—starting with calling off the wedding tomorrow. But once that was done there was a whole new future out there for them.

He was sure of it.

* * *

The sounds of the rehearsal dinner were fading. How many people must have left already without even seeing her? She should have been there, playing hostess, saying goodbye to people, looking excited about tomorrow. If Isabella would let her, of course. She had to start reclaiming that role if she was going to be Flynn's wife. People needed to see that she belonged there, at the head of table, running things.

Image was everything; she was the PR face of Morrison-Ashton and, however much this should have been a private event, it wasn't. These were clients, associates, investors, and she should have been there, working the room. Putting on a show.

And instead she'd been outside on the terrace, sleeping with the best man in the open air.

A shudder ran through her. What had she been thinking? Anyone could have walked out and seen them, and then everything would have been destroyed.

Of course, she reminded herself, it might still be once she told Flynn.

'Thea?' Helena clattered into the hall on her high heels. 'Are you okay? I kept everyone else off the terrace and they're all starting to leave now. Do you want to say goodbye? If not I can cover for you if you want to just go to bed?'

Thea gave her sister a half-smile. 'You take such good care of me.'

Helena shook her head and stepped forward to wrap her arms around Thea's waist. 'Not nearly as good as you take of me.'

Was that true? Thea wasn't sure. She'd stayed, yes, when Helena had needed her, and she'd done the best she could to help her. But she'd never pressed her sister to talk about what had happened, never pushed her to get counselling or other help. Whereas ever since she'd come back, thinner and paler, with her stomach still slightly rounded and hidden under baggy jumpers, Helena had made looking out for Thea a priority. She'd been there when her engagements had gone bad, she'd helped Isabella look after the house and Dad while Thea got on with climbing the corporate ladder, she'd smoothed out every difficult conversation, every awkward dinner party between the Morrisons and the Ashtons.

And tonight she'd protected Thea's privacy while she made another huge mistake.

'I need to talk to Flynn.'

Helena pulled back, frowning. 'Are you sure? Now?'

'Yes. Before I lose my nerve.'

'What are you going to tell him?' Helena asked.

Thea wondered how much her sister knew about her and Zeke. What Zeke had told her. What she imagined had happened out on the terrace.

Thea took a breath. 'Everything.'

Helena studied her for a long moment, then nodded. 'Okay, then. I'll fetch him. You go and wait in the library, yeah?'

'Okay.'

The library was shaded and dark, the tiny haloes of light around the table lamps barely enough to illuminate the chairs beside them, let alone the bookcases. Thea trailed her fingers across the shelves, waiting for Flynn, trying not to listen to the sounds of the guests leaving.

Helena's tinkling laugh caught her attention, though. 'She's been up since dawn! She's so excited about tomorrow. I think she's just crashed! I sent her to bed when she couldn't stop yawning. Can't have the bride looking anything but well rested on her wedding day, can we?'

Murmurs of amused agreement from the departing guests made Thea wince. How many lies had Helena told for her tonight?

The library door cracked open, and Thea spun away from the bookshelf.

'Thea?' Flynn asked, his voice as calm and even as it always was. 'Are you in here?'

Stepping into the light, Thea tried to smile. 'I'm here.'

Flynn closed the door carefully behind him with a click, then turned to her. 'Are you okay? Helena said you wanted to talk to me. I'd have come sooner, but our guests...'

Thea winced again. 'Yeah, sorry. I should have been there to talk with them. To say goodbye, at least.'

'Where were you?' Flynn asked. 'Helena's telling everyone you went to bed, but to be honest you don't look that tired. You look... I don't know...'

But Thea did. Her jaw tightened as she imagined what she must look like. Her hair would be rumpled, her dress creased, her make-up faded. She wished the library had a mirror for her to assess the damage. And maybe, a small part of her insisted, to see if she had that same glow, same radiance, that truly great sex with Zeke had always given her.

She kind of hoped not. She couldn't imagine that was something any man would want to see on his fiancée's face if he hadn't put it there. Even someone as affable and not in love with her as Flynn.

'I was on the terrace,' Thea said. 'With Zeke.'

'But Helena said…' Flynn's face hardened. 'Helena lied. What's going on, Thea?'

'I…I need to tell you some things.' Pacing over to the reading area, Thea placed her hands on the back of one leather wingback chair, her fingernails pressing into the leather. 'Perhaps you should sit.'

'You too, then,' Flynn said, motioning at her chair. When she hesitated, he added, 'Come on, Thea, you look like you're about to fall over.'

Thea slipped around and sat down, instantly regretting it as the stupid table lamp that gave only a glow to the rest of the room illuminated her completely. She could feel the light on her face and see the lamp opposite doing the same to Flynn's as he took his seat. It felt as if she was sitting in an interrogation room, which really didn't give her a good feeling about how the rest of this conversation was going to go.

'So…' Flynn said. 'Talk.'

She should have asked for a drink. Should have stolen the rest of the champagne she'd left outside with Zeke. Should have stayed at her rehearsal dinner if she was going to rewrite the evening.

Instead she took a breath and searched her mind for where to begin.

'Eight years ago,' she said—because wasn't that when everything had started?—'when Zeke left… he asked me to go with him.'

'Why?'

'Because we were in love.' Facts, even painful ones, were the only way to do this. The only way to make Flynn understand what had happened tonight.

Flynn shifted in his chair. 'I should have brought whisky.'

'Yeah. Sorry.'

'So. You didn't go with him. Why?'

'Because…' Could she tell him? It was Helena's secret. She'd told Zeke, but that had been her choice. Flynn deserved the truth… In the end she plumped for the simplified version. 'Helena needed me. She was sixteen, and she had a lot of stuff going on in her life. Our mother had died… she needed me. I couldn't leave her.'

'But if it hadn't been for Helena?'

The million-dollar question. 'I don't know.' Except she did—in her heart. 'Zeke and I…we're very different people. Especially these days.'

'Okay. So what does this all have to do with tonight?'

Heat flooded Thea's cheeks as the shame of her actions hit home. 'I slept with Zeke tonight.'

'On the terrace? Where anyone could see?' Flynn's eyebrows shot up. 'That…doesn't sound very like you.'

Thea blinked at him. '*That's* your concern?'

Flynn sighed. 'Thea, I'm not an idiot. I knew the moment Zeke came back that there was unfinished business between you. I guess I was away at university when he left, so maybe I didn't know the ins and outs of it then. But seeing the two of you together this week, seeing how you act around me when he's there…neither of you are exactly subtle, Thea.'

'Oh. Okay.' Thea swallowed around the lump

that had formed in her throat. 'Do you…do you hate me?'

Flynn's smile was gentle, far gentler than she deserved, and tears stung at Thea's eyes. 'Of course I don't hate you, Thea…' He sighed. 'Look. We know this isn't a love match. We're not married yet, so the fidelity clause isn't in effect.'

She'd forgotten all about that clause. One moment of Zeke's hands on her skin and she'd lost all reason.

'Quite honestly, if you have doubts like this and things you need to resolve, I'd far rather them happen now than in a year's time.'

'So…what happens now?'

'Well, that's up to you.' Flynn sat back in his chair and studied her. 'You need to decide what you want, Thea. If you think you could be truly happy with Zeke, that he can give you everything you need, then we'll go and talk to our parents and call the wedding off right now. But if you want the life we have planned—the business, the family support, kids, everything—if you still want that, then you need to forget about Zeke and marry me tomorrow.'

Thea stared at him, waiting for something

more—something to make the choice for her, to make sure she made the right one. To tell her the right answer to this test.

But Flynn didn't offer advice. Didn't counsel… didn't help her reason it out. He just sat there and watched her. How could he be so impassive? But then, she'd wanted businesslike, detached, practical. She hadn't wanted Flynn to love her. He was giving her exactly what she'd always said she needed. And, against all the odds, she was still enough for him. She could still give him what he wanted, too, even knowing how much she'd messed up.

'It has to be your choice, Thea,' he said.

And, worst of all, she knew he was right.

CHAPTER TEN

'ARE YOU OKAY out here?'

Zeke turned at the sound of Helena's voice and saw the concerned crumple of her forehead as she stood in the door, watching him.

'I'm fine.' He patted the swing seat beside him. 'Wanna sit? Your sister has left us a little of the champagne.' He thought it wise not to mention exactly how Thea had been distracted from the champagne, right there on that very swing.

But Helena didn't sit anyway. Instead she leant against the railing opposite and reached out a hand for the bottle. Her high heels had been discarded, Zeke realised, and she seemed far smaller than the loss of a few inches should achieve.

'Everything okay in there?' he asked as Helena lifted the bottle to her lips. Of course what he really wanted to ask was, *Where's Thea? How did Flynn take it? When is she coming back?*

'Fine,' Helena said, passing the bottle back. 'The

guests have all gone, or retired to their rooms. Thea and Flynn are in the library, talking. Your dad's in the study, and Isabella and Dad are sipping brandy in the back parlour, I think.'

That strange split again, Zeke thought. Everyone with the wrong person. Mum with Thomas, Thea with Flynn, and him out here with Helena.

'Do you know what they're talking about?' he asked.

Helena raised her eyebrows. 'Dad and Isabella? I dread to think.'

'I meant Thea and Flynn.' Zeke paused. 'And why dread to think?'

'Who knows what those two find to talk about?' Helena shrugged, but the look in her eyes told him there was more to it than a weird choice of phrase.

'Helena. What am I missing here?'

She tilted her head to look at him. '*Are* you missing it, though? Or just pretending you don't see it, like Thea?'

'I've been gone for eight years, Helena. I might have missed some stuff.' But he suspected. Always had. And the horrible certainty was already rising up in his gut.

'I knew when I was fourteen,' she replied.

How much more of life had Helena seen before she was an adult? What else had she been doing while Flynn had been at university and he and Thea had been sneaking around thinking that they were being so clever that no one knew about them?

'Knew what?' Zeke asked, even though he was sure he didn't want to know the answer.

'That my father and your mother were having an affair.'

Zeke grabbed the champagne bottle and drank deeply. 'Knew or suspected?' he asked, after wiping his mouth. Because *he'd* suspected, even when he hadn't wanted to. And he'd been very careful not to look any closer just in case he was proved right.

'Knew.'

Helena looked him straight in the eye, as if she wanted to prove the truth of her words.

'I saw them once. And once I'd seen…it was so obvious. I saw the proof of it in every single thing they did. It was a relief, in a way. At least I understood at last why Isabella was so determined to try and be my mother.'

'Yeah.' It explained a lot, even while Zeke

wished that it didn't. What a mess. Tipping his head back against the wall behind the swing, he let his mind rerun the memories of twenty-one years of watching them but not seeing. Helena was right. Once you knew it was impossible not to see.

Was that how people had been with him and Thea?

The thought made him sit bolt-upright. 'Why are you telling me this now? I mean, there's no chance that I'm...' He couldn't even finish the sentence.

Helena's eyes widened. 'Our half-brother? God, no! That's...' She shuddered. 'No. Mum was still alive then, and I'm pretty sure it didn't start until after her death. Besides, Zeke, you look exactly like Ezekiel Senior. I don't think there's ever been any doubt about who your father is.'

'True.' Zeke's muscles relaxed just a little. 'Funny. For years I hated how much of him I saw when I looked in the mirror. Now...I'm profoundly grateful.'

'Hell, yes.'

'So why tell me now?'

Helena paused, her lower lip caught between her teeth. Suddenly she looked like the naughty schoolgirl he remembered, not the poised, sophisticated woman he'd found when he returned. Where had she gone, that Helena? Had all her rough edges and inappropriate comments been smoothed out by the things that had happened to her? By all the secrets she'd had to keep buried? He'd seen a glimpse of her at dinner, though, winding his mother up about the pearls. Maybe she wasn't gone for ever. He hoped not.

'Did you ever wonder why Isabella stayed with your dad?'

Zeke blinked. He hadn't, he realised. But he should have. 'I guess the money. The family. The business.'

'But if she'd left him for *my* dad…'

'They'd have had all of that, to some degree.' And Zeke would have grown up with Thomas Morrison as his stepfather. He really couldn't be sure if that would have been an improvement, or not.

'Yeah.'

'So why?'

Helena shrugged. 'I don't know. I never asked. But maybe somebody should.'

'Why?' What did it matter now, anyway? He'd

be gone tomorrow—leaving all this behind for his future with Thea.

'Because…' Helena took a deep breath. 'Because I think Thea is about to make the same mistake.'

Zeke's world froze. 'No. She's not. She's in there right now, telling Flynn she can't marry him.'

Helena's gaze was sad and sympathetic. 'Are you sure?'

'Yes,' Zeke lied. 'I'm absolutely sure.'

Isabella was waiting for her outside the library when Thea finally left Flynn alone with the books and headed for bed. It wouldn't do for the bride to look tired and distraught on her wedding day, after all. Just as Helena had said.

'Oh, my dear,' Isabella said, clasping her hands together at the sight of her. 'Come on. We'll go and have some tea.'

'Really, Isabella, I'm fine.' The last thing she wanted after the surrealism of her evening so far was to sit and sip tea with her future mother-in-law. 'I just need to get some sleep. It's been a long day.'

But Isabella wasn't taking no for an answer. 'You'll never sleep like this. Come on. Tea.'

Dutifully Thea trailed behind her, wondering how much longer this day could feasibly get. It had to be past midnight already. Even if the wedding wasn't until tomorrow afternoon she couldn't imagine she'd actually get a lie-in, whatever happened. Apart from anything else she still had to talk to Zeke. Flynn had insisted she did, before making any final decisions.

The kitchens were in darkness, the last of the staff having gone home at last. The dishwashers were still running, though, so Thea suspected it had been a late night for all concerned. Isabella found the light switch without difficulty and flicked it on, before heading unerringly for a cupboard which, when opened, revealed a stock of different varieties of tea.

'Camomile?' she asked, glancing back at Thea. Then she frowned. 'Or maybe peppermint. Good for soothing the stomach.'

'My stomach is fine,' Thea replied. It was just her mind that was spinning and her heart that was breaking.

'As you say.' Isabella selected a tin then, opening another cupboard, pulled out a small silver teapot and two fragile-looking cups and saucers.

'I always make it my first priority to locate the teapot, wherever I'm staying. I just can't sleep without a soothing cup of something before bed.'

'I didn't know that.' Thea watched Isabella as she pottered over to the sink to fill the kettle then, while it was boiling, selected a couple of teaspoons and a tea strainer and stand from another drawer.

'Now, Thea…' Isabella placed the tea tray, complete with lace cloth, onto the kitchen table and took a chair opposite her. 'I want to talk to you about Zeke.'

'About Zeke?' Thea's fingers slipped on the handle of the teapot and she pulled back. She should let Isabella pour, anyway.

'Yes. I know you've always been…close to my son.'

'Your husband already asked me to talk to him about This Minute,' Thea interjected, wishing she didn't sound as if she was babbling so much. 'And I tried—I did—but no dice. I think tomorrow he plans to leave and sell to Glasshouse, regardless of what we offer.'

'That's interesting,' Isabella said. 'But not what I wanted to talk about.'

'Then…what? Did you want to know where he's been? Because I have a pretty good idea, I think. Or what his plans are now? Because you'd really have to ask him, except…'

Except he was probably still waiting for her on the terrace. Did he know what she'd planned to tell Flynn? Or did he hope…? No. She couldn't think about it.

'I wanted to talk about your relationship with him. And my relationship with your father.'

Thea blinked. 'I don't understand.'

'Then you haven't been paying very close attention.' Isabella reached for the teapot and, placing the strainer over Thea's cup, started to pour. 'This should be brewed by now.'

'What exactly *is* your relationship with my father?' Thea asked, even though she suspected she already knew the answer. Should have known it for years.

'What exactly is *your* relationship with my youngest son?' Isabella didn't even look up from pouring the tea into her own cup as she turned the question round on Thea.

'I haven't seen him in eight years,' Thea said. 'I

think that any relationship we did have will have been legally declared dead by now.'

'Except he was the one who came after you when you were upset tonight. And I suspect he's the one who's left you looking like your whole world is upside down.'

'Tell me about you and Dad.'

Placing the pot back on the tray, Isabella picked up her teacup and saucer and sat back, surveying Thea over the rim of her steaming cup. 'I think, in some ways, our situation is very similar, you know.'

'I *don't* know,' Thea said. 'I don't know what you're talking about.'

'After your mother died your father was a wreck. I tried to help out where I could. And then, after that nastiness with Helena…'

'You saw your chance and pushed me out,' Thea said, her hackles rising. But Isabella merely raised her eyebrows a few millimetres as she sipped her tea.

'I did what was needed to keep things…settled.'

Sending Helena away and taking over Thea's home. Smoothing over the rough edges of the actual truth and providing a glossy finish. Thea shook her head. 'I don't see how this applies to me and Zeke.'

'Wait,' Isabella said. 'Drink your tea and listen. Over time, your father and I grew close. We talked a lot. We listened a lot. That was something we both needed. You might not have noticed, but my husband is not one of the world's great listeners and his only subject of conversation is the company. It was…different with Thomas.'

Thea's hands tightened around the warmth of her teacup. 'You fell in love.'

'We did. Very deeply.'

No wonder her father had chosen Isabella over her. For the first time Thea saw her past through new eyes. No, she hadn't been up to the job her father had thrown her into. But maybe that had been because it was a role that was never meant to be hers. Maybe he'd wanted Isabella there at his side all along.

Except he'd never got all of her, had he?

'You never left Ezekiel.'

'I never even considered it,' Isabella said without pause. 'And your father never asked me to.'

'Why?'

Isabella sighed. 'Because I was old enough and

wise enough, by the time I fell in love for real, to know that love isn't everything. Thea, we all need different things in this life. Yes, we need someone to listen to us, to laugh with, to love. But we need other things, too.'

'Like money,' Thea guessed, not hiding the bitterness in her voice. How different might her life have been with Isabella as a real stepmother rather than someone who had to help out because Thea couldn't manage things on her own? 'Dad could have given you that, too, you know.'

'Not just money. Yes, Thomas could have given me that—and stability, and lots of other things. But what about the business? What about our social standing? My place in the world? What about Ezekiel and the vows I made?'

'You mean, what about the scandal?' Thea shook her head. 'Is that what it's always about with you? Was this just Helena all over again?'

'All I am saying is there are many aspects of a woman's life for which she has needs. You need to look at your requirements over the course of a lifetime when you're making a decision about whom to marry.'

'And Ezekiel gave you what you needed over

the course of your lifetime? Because, if so, why did you feel the need to have an affair with my father?'

Isabella sipped at her tea delicately before responding. 'That's what I'm saying. Did it ever occur to you that perhaps it is unreasonable to expect one person to fulfil your every need?'

'No.' The response was instinctive, automatic. Even if she were willing to contemplate such a thing, neither Zeke nor Flynn was the sort of man who liked to share.

Isabella gave her a sad smile. 'You're young. You're still holding out for the dream. So, which of my sons do you think can give you that?'

Thea had no answer to that at all.

'If that's the way you feel you have only two options,' Isabella said. 'One: you marry Flynn as planned. Everyone is happy and no one needs to be any the wiser about your…indiscretion. You go about your life and probably never see Zeke again.'

'What's option two?' Thea asked, her mouth dry.

'You call off the wedding and leave with Zeke. You leave behind your career, your family and reputation, your chance at a stable and loving future, for a man who has already left you behind once. In an effort to put a good face on the company my husband will probably marry Flynn off to someone else pretty quickly. Helena, I imagine, would be the best candidate.'

'No.' The very idea chilled Thea's core. 'She wouldn't.'

'She would,' Isabella replied, with certainty in her voice. 'She couldn't bear to let everyone down *again*. Besides, surely you've noticed the way she looks at him.'

'No.'

Was Isabella just saying that to convince her to marry Flynn? Didn't she know that if she'd thought Helena wanted him she'd step aside in an instant? Probably not. Isabella had spent so many years watching Ezekiel drive a wedge between her sons she probably believed everyone wanted what their sibling had.

'I'd look closer, then.'

Thea shook her head. 'You're imagining things, Isabella. And it doesn't matter anyway.'

'Oh? Have you found a magical third path, then? Other than my original suggestion?'

'No.' Thea stared down into her teacup. If she was honest, she'd known all along what she really had to do. For her future and for her family. 'I'll marry Flynn, just as we've always planned.'

Isabella watched her for a long moment, then nodded. 'Good. Now, more tea?'

'No. Thank you.' Thea pushed her chair away from the table and stood. 'I need to go to bed. Lots to do tomorrow.'

Starting with explaining her decision to the one person in the world who would never, ever understand it.

Zeke woke early the next morning. He'd waited up for Thea on the terrace until he'd realised all the lights inside had been turned off. Helena had kept vigil with him for a while, before patting him on the shoulder and bidding him goodnight. When he'd finally given up and gone to bed he'd lingered outside Thea's door for long moments, contemplating knocking and going in. But Thea had to make this decision for herself—even he knew that much.

In the end he'd headed to bed alone, for a night of restless dreams and uncertainty. And now it was the morning of Thea and Flynn's wedding, and he still didn't know her decision.

From the moment he woke he felt panic surge through him at the realisation that he was alone again. Why hadn't she come? He'd been so sure... Flynn must have said something. Threatened her, perhaps... Except that wasn't his style. No, he'd have baffled her with logic. Probably had a spreadsheet of reasons they should get married as planned.

Just what Thea didn't need.

Sitting up in bed, Zeke stamped down on the fear creeping across his brain and contemplated his next move. He could still fix this, still win, if he played the right hand. Did he wait for Thea to come to him, or did he seek her out? There was always the chance that she might not come at all. If she'd made her decision—the wrong decision—what would be the point? But Zeke knew he couldn't live with the not knowing.

So what other choice did he have? He could just cut his losses now. He could go and say goodbye to Thea, give her one last chance to go with him, then leave if she said no.

In the end the choice wasn't his or Thea's. As

he exited his bedroom, freshly showered and ca-sually dressed—no way was he getting stuck in a tux this early in the day, even if the wedding went ahead and he actually attended—he saw Flynn, marching towards him.

'You and I need to talk,' his adopted brother said, face solemn. 'And then you need to talk to Thea.'

'Okay.' Zeke fell into step with Flynn, his heart rising slightly in his chest. Maybe he wouldn't need to convince Thea again after all. If Flynn wanted him to talk to her surely that meant he didn't approve of her decision. Well, he was damned if he thought Zeke would try to persuade her otherwise. 'What exactly do we need to talk about?'

Flynn gave him an exasperated look. 'Thea, of course.'

'Right.'

Zeke waited until Flynn had yanked open the door to the library and impatiently motioned him in before asking any more questions. Settling down into a wingback chair, he suddenly remembered Helena's words from the night before. This was where Flynn and Thea had talked after the interlude on the terrace. How he wished he could have heard what they'd said…

Maybe Flynn would tell him. If he asked right.

'So,' Zeke said, folding one leg up to rest his ankle on the opposite knee. 'What's up? Last-minute nerves?'

Flynn glared at him. 'In precisely six hours I'm supposed to marry Thea. If you have any interest at all in that event, however twisted, you need to stop playing *now*. I need you to be my brother, for once, and I need you to be honest with me.'

Zeke flinched under his brother's gaze. How had he become the kid brother again, the screw-up, the one who couldn't be serious about anything that mattered? Especially when he'd worked so hard to get away from that. Away from the bitter rivalry for something that had turned out not to matter at all—their father's approval.

'Fine. Then talk.'

'Thea told me that she slept with you last night.'

'She said she was going to.' Zeke looked Flynn right in the eye as he talked. He wasn't ashamed, even if he should be. Thea belonged with *him*, not in some soulless, loveless marriage of con-

venience. Getting her out of that was not a sin.
Trapping her was.

'I still plan to marry her.'

'For the love of God, *why*?' Zeke grabbed the
arms of the chair and sat forward. What else did
he have to *do*? 'You don't love her—I know you
don't. You couldn't be this calm right now if you
did. And she doesn't love you!'

'Do you think she's still in love with you?'

'I know she is. And I know she deserves a lot
better than what you have to offer.'

'And what, exactly, are *you* offering?' Flynn
asked, staring at Zeke. 'The chance to say *screw
you* to our father?'

'That's not...' Zeke sank back down into his
chair. 'That's not why.'

'Are you sure?' Flynn tilted his head as he considered his brother. 'It's been eight years, Zeke.
Why come back now, if not to prove a point?'

'Oh, I don't know—maybe to stop Thea making a huge mistake.'

'And you think you're the best judge of Thea's
mistakes?'

'Better than her, at least,' Zeke said, thinking

about Helena and all the guilt Thea carried on her behalf.

Flynn shook his head. 'You're wrong. But I told Thea last night she had to decide for herself what to do. I told her to think about it overnight, then talk to us both this morning. She'll be here any minute.'

And just like that the decision about how to approach Thea was taken away from him.

'Good,' Zeke said, hoping his surprise didn't show on his face.

He didn't want to have this conversation in front of his brother. Flynn made him a different person even now, after all these years. He needed it to be just him and Thea, so they could just be themselves, the people he remembered so well. But apparently his love life was now in the public domain. And before he could even object the library door opened and Thea was standing there, looking pale and lovely—and determined.

Zeke stood up. Time to win this.

CHAPTER ELEVEN

THEA SUCKED IN a breath as she opened the library door and saw Zeke and Flynn waiting for her. This was it. The moment that decided the rest of her life. Whatever she'd told Isabella, whatever she'd told herself in the dark of the night, her decision couldn't be final until she'd told the two men in this room. This might be the biggest choice and possibly the biggest mistake she'd ever made as an adult. So of course it involved Zeke Ashton.

'Thea, you're here. Good.'

Flynn gave her a gentle smile that made Thea's insides tie up in knots. She didn't want to be there *so much*.

But she was, and she was out of other options, so she moved to the centre of the room and took the chair Flynn indicated. This was his condition: he'd marry her today if she talked things through with both of them and still decided it was the best option. Since she'd slept with someone else the night before their wedding, Thea had to admit that this was more than fair. That was the thing about Flynn. He was always scrupulously fair. Even when she wanted him to just yell, or walk out, or make a decision for her.

'Okay, so here's what I'm thinking.' Flynn settled into his own chair, looking for all the world as if this was an everyday meeting or discussion. As if they weren't debating whether or not to get *married* that afternoon. 'We all know the situation. And we all agree that Thea has to be the one to make a decision about what happens next—correct?'

He glanced between them, focussing first on Zeke, who eventually nodded in a way that made it very clear he was doing so under duress, and then at Thea, who whispered, 'Yes,' even though she didn't want to.

'So… I think the best way to proceed is—'

'Oh, for God's sake!' Zeke interrupted. 'This isn't a board meeting, Flynn.'

'No,' Flynn replied, his voice calm and even. 'It's a meeting about my future. And since you're the one who's put that into the realm of uncertainty, I think you should just let me deal with it my own way, don't you?'

Zeke settled back into his chair at that, and Thea risked a glance over at him. His eyes were dark and angry, and she could see the tension in his hands, in the way they gripped the arms of the chair, even if his posture was relaxed. How he must hate this—must hate waiting to see if Flynn was going to beat him again. Because of course that was how Zeke would see it, even if it wasn't true. This wasn't about either of them, really, even if only Flynn seemed to realise that.

It was about Thea. About her making the right decision for once. Whatever that might be.

'So, here's what I propose,' Flynn said, and Thea tried to concentrate on listening to him instead of watching the way Zeke's jaw tightened with every word. 'Zeke and I will both lay out our arguments for why we feel you should choose our proposed course of action. You can listen, ask questions, and then we'll leave you alone to make your decision. The only thing I ask is that you decide quickly; once guests start arriving it will be a lot harder to cancel this thing, if you choose to.'

Thea nodded, and stopped looking at Zeke altogether.

'Okay. Shall I go first?' Flynn asked, and when no one answered he continued, 'Right. Thea, obviously I want to marry you today. I understand what happened last night, and I think, after talking with you yesterday, I can see why. But I don't believe that one impulsive action has to change the course of your whole life. We agreed to a contract—a marriage between us based on very sound reasoning and mutual desires. Everything we discussed and decided still stands. I can give you the security, the business, the future that you want. And marriage is only a small part of our lives; we have to consider the other people we love—what *they* want. I think we both know that everyone in this villa except Zeke wants a future with us as a couple in it. We can do so much together, Thea. And, quite honestly, I'd worry about your future if you left with Zeke today.'

He got up from the chair and came to stand by her side, gently taking her hand in his.

'Because, Thea, I care about you. Maybe we don't have that grand passion. But we have more. Mutual respect, caring, common interests and values. They matter too. And I suggest to you, right here, that they matter more for what we want to achieve in life.'

He wasn't just thinking about the business, Thea realised. He was talking about kids. Flynn would be a great father—calm and fair. And she was pretty sure he wouldn't ever sleep with his best friend's wife. Unlike her own father. Unlike Zeke, she thought, stealing a glance at him. Hell, he'd slept with her the night before her wedding. Morality had never been a strong motivation for him.

Or for her this week, it seemed.

Flynn seemed to be waiting for an answer, so Thea nodded and said, 'That all makes a lot of sense,' even though her poor muddled brain could barely remember what he'd said.

Maybe it didn't matter, she realised. Maybe, whatever they each had to say, it all meant nothing in the end. She couldn't weigh up the pros and cons of two people, could she?

Except she had to. And not just of the two men in front of her but of the whole lives they represented. She could see two futures for herself, branching off from this moment, and she simply didn't know which one was more terrifying.

But she still had to decide.

Flynn gave a sharp nod, then moved away to his own chair, yielding the floor to his brother. 'Zeke. Your turn.'

Zeke looked up slowly, his dark gaze finally meeting hers. 'I don't know what you want me to say.'

'Neither do I,' Thea admitted. Did she want him to talk her out of marrying Flynn—really? Or did she want him to say something so awful that she stopped feeling guilty about marrying Zeke's brother in the first place? She wasn't sure.

He blew out a long breath. 'Okay. I don't want you to marry Flynn. I think it's a mistake.'

Thea flinched at the word, even though she tried not to. 'It's mine to make, though.'

'It is,' Zeke conceded. 'I just… I really don't want to do this with him in the room.'

'He's your brother. And he's right—he does have kind of a big stake in this conversation.'

'I know.' Zeke took another breath. 'Okay, fine. I know you think you're doing this for the family, to prove yourself to them somehow. And I know you believe that everyone will be happy if you just go along with their plans. But you're wrong.'

'And our happiness is suddenly of such importance to you? Zeke, you haven't cared about us for the last eight years. I find it hard to believe that we suddenly matter that much to you.'

'Of course I've cared!' Zeke yelled, and Flynn's gaze shot to the door, as if he was worrying about who might be listening. It was a fear that seemed all the more reasonable when Zeke's words were followed by a knock on the library door a moment later.

'Ah, here you all are,' Isabella said, giving them all her best hostess smile. 'Thea, darling, there's a small question about the table settings that we could use your input on, if you have a moment.'

Isabella's eyes were knowing, but Thea refused to meet them.

'I'll deal with it,' Flynn said, getting to his feet. 'Thea and Zeke are just reminiscing about old times, Mother. Something they won't have much of a chance to do once we're married.'

She had to know it was a lie, but Isabella let it go nonetheless. 'Come on, then. And once this is sorted, perhaps you can help me with the question of the gift table.'

Flynn shut the door firmly behind them, and

Thea felt as if he'd taken all the air in the room with him. Now it was just her and Zeke and every moment of their history, weighing down on them like the books on the shelves.

'That's better,' Zeke said. 'Now we can do this properly.'

How could she look so poised and calm, when he felt as if his insides were about to combust? For Thea this might as well be just another business meeting. Maybe she was a perfect match for Flynn after all.

No. If this was his last chance to try and uncover the Thea he'd known and loved, the one he'd glimpsed again as he'd made love to her on the terrace last night, then he was grasping it with both hands. He had to make her see sense.

'Maybe we should wait until Flynn gets back,' Thea said, as if she truly believed that any part of this discussion really did involve his brother.

'This isn't about Flynn,' Zeke said. 'He could be anyone. Any poor bloke you'd roped in to try and make your life safe and predictable. Just like the last two. No, this is about you and me, and it always has been.'

Thea's gaze shot up to meet his, dark and heated. 'You mean it's all about *you*. You proving a point to your father. Just like it always is.'

'Last night wasn't just about me,' Zeke replied, enjoying the flush of red that ran up her neck to her cheeks. 'In fact I distinctly remember it being all about you more than once.'

'This isn't about sex, Zeke,' Thea snapped. 'This is my future you're playing with.'

'Who said I'm playing?' Because he wasn't—not one bit. He knew exactly how important this moment was. But with Thea sometimes you had to get her mad to see the truth. To let her true self break out from all the rules and restrictions she'd tucked herself in with like a safety blanket.

Thea gave a bitter laugh. 'It's always been a game to you—all of it. You've always cared more about beating your father and Flynn than anything else. If you'd paid any attention at all you'd know that Flynn isn't even competing. He's just getting on with his life, like an ordinary, good man.'

'And that's what you want, is it? Ordinary?' If she thought it was, she was wrong. Thea deserved much, much more than ordinary.

'I want to not be a trophy! I want to not be one more thing you can use against your family for some misguided slight almost a decade ago!'

The words hit him hard in the chest. 'That's not what I'm doing.'

'Isn't it? Are you sure? Because it seems to me that coming back here—right when you're about to sell your company to our competitor, just when I'm about to get on and make a success of my life—is far more about you and your need to win than anything else.'

'You're wrong.'

'Prove it.'

'How?'

'I don't know, Zeke! But if you really want me to throw over all my plans for the future, to upset both our families, probably damage the company's reputation…you need to offer me a little more than a cheap victory over your father and one night on a terrace.'

One night. Was that what it was to her? Was that all he'd ever been? A bit of fun, but never the one you chose for the long haul. No wonder she'd stayed eight years ago.

'Helena must have been a real handy excuse

that night,' he said, letting the bitterness creep into his voice.

Thea blinked. 'What?'

'Tell me honestly. If it hadn't been for Helena would you have come with me when I asked, that night of your birthday party?'

The colour faded from Thea's cheeks and he knew the answer before she even spoke the word.

'No.'

Zeke tightened his muscles against the pain, stiffening into strength and resolve. With a sharp nod, he said, 'That's what I thought.'

'I just…I wanted…'

'You don't need to justify yourself to me.' A strange calm had settled over him now. At last he knew, and to his surprise the truth made all the difference. 'I understand.'

'No! You don't,' Thea said, but Zeke just shook his head.

'Sure I do. You want a safe and predictable life, even if it makes you miserable.' How had he thought for so many years that Thea was different from the rest of them? He should have known that they were all the same at heart. More concerned with the appearance of the thing than the substance. Better that he realised that now, however belatedly, than go on believing she was something more than she was.

'That's not… It's not just that,' Thea said unconvincingly.

'Yeah, Thea, it is. Deny it all you want, but I know what's going on here. You're doing exactly what Daddy wants, as usual. You're going to marry Flynn to buy yourself the place you think you deserve.'

She looked away, but Zeke wasn't looking for shame in her expression. It was too late for that now, anyway. She'd made her choice and he knew his future now. But that didn't mean he couldn't open her eyes to a few home truths before he left.

'You realise you could be pregnant with my child already?' They hadn't used protection last night. Had been too caught up in the moment even to think of it.

'I know.'

'Does Flynn?'

'Yes.' A whisper…barely even a word.

'And he's happy to marry you anyway?' Of course he was. In fact he probably hoped that she was. 'Because that would give him the one thing he's never had, wouldn't it? Legitimacy. Raising a true Ashton blood heir with the Morrison heiress. Perfect.'

Thea sprang to her feet to defend her fiancé. 'You don't have a clue what you're talking about! And anyway Flynn *is* the Ashton heir, remember? You gave it all up to run away and seek revenge.'

'Because my father chose him over me!' Zeke couldn't keep the anger from his voice this time. However far he moved past the pain, the sting of unfairness still caught him unawares sometimes.

'Your father made a business choice, not a personal one.'

Zeke flinched at her words. 'You're wrong there,' he said.

'Am I?'

He knew she was, but couldn't bring himself to explain, to argue. To revisit in glorious Technicolor the night he'd left. The things he'd heard his father say. What had really driven him away. Why he'd had to go even when Thea wouldn't leave with him. Why her rejection had been just one more slam to the heart.

What was wrong with him? He'd moved past this years ago. Wasn't that one of the reasons he'd come back in the first place? To prove that he'd moved on, that he had his own life now, that he didn't need his family or the business? So why was he letting her arguments get to him?

Was it the idea of a possible baby? The thought that *his child* might be brought up in the Morrison-Ashton clan, living its whole life waiting to see if it would be deemed *worthy enough* to inherit everything that Zeke had walked away from…? It made him sick to his stomach. No child—no person—deserved to go through that. But what were the honest chances that Thea was pregnant? Slim, he'd imagine. And she'd tell him, he knew. Thea might not be everything he'd thought she was, but she was honest. She'd told Flynn about sleeping with him, hadn't she? She'd tell Zeke if he were a father.

And then he'd be tied into this accursed family for ever. Perfect.

What had he been thinking, sleeping with her last night? Zeke wanted to beat himself up for it, except he knew exactly what he'd been thinking—that he might be able to save Thea from herself this time.

But Thea didn't want to be saved. She'd rejected

him again, and this time it cut even deeper. She'd chosen Flynn. She wanted Flynn.

Fine. She could have him. But Zeke was making sure she knew exactly what she was letting herself in for first.

CHAPTER TWELVE

THEA THOUGHT SHE could bear anything except sitting one moment longer under Zeke's too knowing gaze. Who was he to judge her, to condemn her? To think he knew her better than she knew herself?

Except he just might.

No. She couldn't let herself believe that. After a sleepless night, spent with Flynn and Isabella's words resounding in her brain while her memories ran one long, sensual video of her evening with Zeke, she knew only one thing for certain: she was done with doing what other people said she should. Everyone in the whole villa thought they knew what was best for her, and Zeke was just the latest in a long line.

Well, she was done with it.

'You realise that you're choosing what other people expect of you over what you really want, right?' Zeke said, and she glared at him.

'How would you know what I want? And if you make one single innuendo or reference to last night after that comment I'm walking out right now.'

The smirk on his face told her that was exactly what Zeke had been about to do, but instead he said, 'Because I've seen you do it before, far too many times. You admitted you wouldn't have come with me even if Helena hadn't needed you. But why? I can tell you, even if you don't know yourself.'

Thea rolled her eyes. 'Enlighten me, oh, wise one,' she said, as sarcastically as she could manage.

'Because you're scared. Because you've spent your whole life doing what other people think is best for you and you don't even know how to stop. You can't make peace with your own desires because you think they might upset someone.'

'They upset *me*!' Thea yelled. 'Zeke! Do you think I want to be this person? The sort of woman who sleeps with the best man the night before her wedding? I hate myself right now! The best thing I can do is try and get back to my regularly scheduled life, without the chaos you bring into it. Is that so bad?'

'Not if the regularly scheduled life is what you really want.'

Zeke moved closer, and Thea's body started to hum at his nearness.

'But I don't think it is. I think that you want more. You want a life that makes your heart sing. You want it all.'

He swayed closer again, and before she knew it his hand was at her waist, pulling her towards him, and his lips were dipping towards hers...

She wanted this so badly. Wanted his mouth on hers, his body against her. But she couldn't have it. Not if she wanted all the other things she'd promised herself—her family, security, her work. This was her last chance to get things right—and she had to take it. However tempted she was to give in to desire over sense.

'No, Zeke.' She pushed him away, not letting her palms linger on his chest for a moment longer than necessary. 'I'm marrying Flynn.'

'Then you're a fool.'

Zeke stepped away, turning his back on her, but

not before she saw the flash in his eyes of—what? Anger? Frustration? She couldn't be sure.

'I'm making the sensible decision,' Thea said, even though it felt as if her heart might force its way out of her sensible ribcage at any moment to fight its own case.

'You're making a mistake.'

'Am I?' Thea shook her head. This was going to hurt. And this was going to make him angry. But she needed to say it. Hell, she'd been waiting eight years to tell him this. It was past due. 'What about you? You say I'm relying on other people to tell me how to live, but how are you any better?'

'I live my life exactly the way I want.' Zeke ran his hand through his messy hair as he turned back towards her. 'By my own judgement. No archaic family loyalty rules or duty to manipulative men.'

'Really? Seems to me that everything you've done since you left—hell, even leaving in the first place—has all been more about your father than you.'

Zeke shook his head. 'You don't know what you're talking about.'

'I do,' Thea said firmly. 'Because I know you, Zeke. You said you wanted to leave Morrison-

Ashton and everything it represented behind when you left. But what did you do? You went and worked for another media conglomerate and then set up your own rival company, for heaven's sake!'

'Stick with what you know, and all that,' Zeke said with a shrug, but Thea wasn't listening.

'And now you're here, still trying to prove to everyone that you don't need them. You're still so bitter about your father giving Flynn the job you wanted—'

'It's not just that!'

'You're so bitter,' Thea carried on, 'that you can't move on. I bet even when you were away you were still checking up on your family. People keep saying that you walked out and left us, but you didn't. You've carried us with you every step of the way and, Zeke, that chip on your shoulder is only getting bigger and heavier. And until you let it go you're never going to be happy. Not even if I left with you right now.'

'You're wrong,' Zeke said, but even as he spoke he could feel the truth of her words resonating through his body. 'I'm done with the lot of you for good this time.'

Her smile was sad, but it enraged him. Who was she to tell him the mistakes he was making in his life? Thea Morrison—the queen of bad decisions. And, even if she didn't know it yet, this was the worst one. Well, she'd have a long, miserable marriage during which to regret it.

Zeke might have been willing to take a lot from Thea Morrison, but this was the last. The last rejection he'd ever face from anyone with the surname Morrison or Ashton.

He was done.

His chest ached as he realised this might be the last time he ever saw her. That he was walking away again and she wouldn't be coming with him this time, either. He choked back a laugh as he realised the awful truth. She'd been right all along. She'd been right not to leave with him eight years ago. They *had* been kids. And he knew now that he hadn't even understood what love was then.

He couldn't have loved Thea at eighteen—not really. He hadn't known her the way he did now, for a start. But mostly he knew it had to be true because, however much he'd thought it had hurt to leave her last time, it didn't come close to the pain searing through his body at the thought of leaving her now..

He loved Thea Morrison, the woman she'd grown up to be, more than he'd ever believed possible. And it didn't make a bit of difference.

None of it mattered now. Not their past, not this horrific week in Tuscany, and certainly not their impossible future. When he left this time he wouldn't be coming back. And he knew just how to make sure that every atom of his relationship with these people was left behind too.

'Maybe you don't know it yet,' he said, keeping his voice calm and even, 'but you're going to make yourself, my brother, and everyone else around you desperately unhappy if you go through with this wedding. I love you. And I would have done anything to make you happy. Anything except stay here and live this safe life you think you want. But it will end up driving you mad. One day you're going to wake up and realise all that, and know what a mistake you've made. But, like you say, it's your mistake to make.'

He didn't look back as he walked to the door. He didn't want to see her standing there, beautiful, sad and resolved. She loved him—he knew it. But she wasn't going to let herself have the one thing that could make her happy.

Fine. It was her mistake, as she'd said.

But she couldn't make him watch.

'Goodbye, Thea,' he said as he walked out through the door.

The door shut behind him with a click, although it felt like an earth-shattering slam to Thea. She'd done it. She'd really done it. She'd sent him away, made the right decision for once. Avoided the oh, so tempting mistake she'd made so many times before. She'd won.

So why did she feel so broken?

Sinking into the chair, Thea sat very still and waited for whatever would happen next. The stylist would be here soon, she vaguely remembered, to do her hair and make-up. Helena would come and find her when it was time, wouldn't she? And in the meantime…she'd just wait for someone to tell her what she was supposed to do.

The irony of her thoughts surprised a laugh from her, and she buried her face in her hands before her laughter turned to tears. The decision was made and Zeke would leave now. She could get back to that regularly scheduled life she'd been hankering after for the past three days.

It was over at last.

Hearing a click, she looked up again in time to see the door open. For one fleeting moment her heart jumped at the thought that it might be Zeke, coming back to try and win her one last time. But, really, what else was there to say? They'd both said everything they needed to, everything they'd been holding in for the last eight years. That moment had passed. *Their* moment.

Flynn stuck his head around the door and, seeing she was alone, came in, shutting it behind him.

'Everything okay?' he asked, hovering nervously at a distance.

Poor Flynn. The things she'd put him through this week… He was such a good man. He didn't deserve it.

So she tried very hard to smile as she looked up at him, to make him feel wanted and loved. To feel like the winner he'd turned out to be. Her man, her choice, her future. Now and always.

'Fine,' she said, her cheeks aching. 'But I'm afraid you're going to need a new best man.'

The look of relief on his face was almost reward enough. 'I think I can arrange that.'

He moved towards her, settling on the arm of her chair, one hand at her shoulder in a comforting fatherly gesture. He'd be a brilliant dad, Thea thought again. It was important to focus on all the excellent reasons she had for marrying him, rather than the one uncertain and confusing reason not to.

'Are you okay?' Flynn asked, and Thea nodded.

'I'm fine. It was…a little difficult, that's all.'

'And you're sure you want to go through with this today? I mean, I appreciate you choosing me, Thea, I really do. And I think it's the right decision. We're going to have a great future together, I know. But it doesn't have to start today—not if you don't want. We could postpone—'

'No,' Thea interrupted. 'I've made my choice. I want to do this.'

Before she changed her mind.

Zeke didn't knock on his father's office door. He didn't need permission or approval from his father for what was going to happen next. In fact he didn't need anything from him. That was sort of the point.

Ezekiel Ashton looked up as Zeke walked in, and his eyebrows rose in amused interest. 'Zeke. Shouldn't you be off practising your best man's speech somewhere?'

'I believe that by now Flynn will have chosen a better man.' Zeke dropped into the visitor's chair, slouching casually. 'I'll be leaving as soon as I'm packed.'

Guests would start arriving soon, he was sure, for the pre-wedding drinks reception that Isabella had insisted on when she'd discovered that Thea planned a late afternoon wedding. He could probably grab one of the taxis bringing people up from the hotel to get him to the airport. He'd call his assistant while he packed and get her to book a flight.

This time tomorrow he'd be in another country. Another life.

'You're not staying, then.' Ezekiel shook his head sadly and turned his attention back to his paperwork. 'I don't know why I'm surprised.'

He doesn't matter. Nothing he thinks or does matters to me any more.

'I have one piece of business to conclude with you before I go,' Zeke said, watching in amusement as he became of interest to his father again.

'Oh, yes? I was under the impression that the very idea of doing business with your own father was distasteful to you.'

'It is,' Zeke said bluntly. 'But it has come to my attention that it may be the only way to sever my ties with you for good.'

'You make it sound so violent,' Ezekiel said. 'When really all you're doing is running away from your responsibilities. And, Zeke, we all know that you'll come back again eventually. We're family. That's what you do for family.'

Zeke shook his head. 'Not this one. Do you know why I left eight years ago?'

'Because you felt slighted that I'd given a position you considered rightfully yours to your brother.'

'No.' Zeke thought back to that horrible day and for the first time felt a strange detachment from the events. 'Because I finally understood why you'd done it. I heard you that day, talking to Thomas about us. I'd come to talk to you about you giving Flynn my job—the one I'd always been promised. I had all these arguments ready...' He shook his head at the memory of his righteous younger self. 'I heard you laugh and say that you realised now that perhaps it wasn't such a misfortune that Mum had fallen pregnant twenty-one years ago, just as Flynn's adoption was confirmed. That while you hadn't planned for two children perhaps it had all been for the best after all.'

He'd stood frozen outside his father's office door, Zeke remembered, his hand half raised to knock. And he'd listened as his father had ruined his relationship with his brother for good.

'This way,' Ezekiel had said, 'they have built-in competition. In some ways it's better, having two sons. Flynn has always felt he has to earn his place, so he fights for it—he fights to belong every day. And as long as I let Zeke feel that he's the disappointment, the second son, he'll keep fighting to best his brother. It's a perfect set-up.'

'"I've told Zeke I've given Flynn the position as my right-hand man,"' you said.' Zeke watched the memory dawning in his father's eyes. '"Of course Zeke will get the company one day. But I want him to fight his brother for it, first."'

The words still echoed in Zeke's skull—the moment his whole life had made horrifying, unbelievable sense, and everything he'd ever thought he wanted had ceased to matter. He'd had to leave—had to get away. And so he'd run straight to Thea and asked her to go with him, only to have his world, his expectations, damned again. That one night had changed his whole life.

'Do you remember saying that, *Dad*?'

Ezekiel nodded. 'Of course I do. And what of it? Healthy competition is good for the soul.'

'That wasn't healthy. Nothing you did to us was *healthy*.'

Zeke leant forward in his chair, gripping the armrests tightly to stop himself standing and pacing. He wanted to look his father in the eye as he told him this.

'What you did to us was unfair at best, cruel at worst. You pitted two people who should have been friends, brothers, against each other. You drove a wedge between us from the moment we were born. You made me feel rejected, inadequate. And you made Flynn believe that he had to fight for every scrap from the table. You drove your wife into the arms of your best friend, you drove me to the other end of the country, and you drove Flynn and Thea to believe that marrying each other is the only way to serve the family business, to earn their place in the family. You are a manipulative, cold, uncaring man and *I am done with you.*'

Ezekiel was silent at his words, but Zeke didn't bother looking for remorse in his expression. He wouldn't find it, and even if by some miracle he did it didn't matter now.

'I am here today to undertake my final act of business with you, old man,' Zeke said, relaxing back in the chair. 'I am going to sell you This Minute, for twice what Glasshouse were offering.' He scribbled down the figure and pushed the scrap of paper across the table.

Ezekiel read it and nodded. 'I knew you'd see sense about this in the end.'

'I'm not done,' Zeke said. 'That's just the financial cost. I want something more.'

'A position at the company?' Ezekiel guessed. 'Would Director of Digital Media suffice for now?'

'I don't want a job. I never wanted to work for you in the first place. I want you to give Thea that role. I want you to make sure she has the freedom to run it her way, and to make her own mistakes. You cannot interfere one iota.'

Ezekiel gave a slow nod. 'That should be possible. As her father always says, her business decisions are far more credible than her personal ones. And she's due a promotion once the wedding is over.'

Zeke knew this game. By the time he left Ezekiel would have convinced himself that Thea's new job had been all his idea in the first place.

He'd have a harder time doing that with his second demand, Zeke wagered.

'One more thing,' Zeke said, and waited until he had his father's full attention before he continued. 'I want you to step down and appoint Flynn as the CEO of Morrison-Ashton. You can take a year for the handover,' he said, talking over his father's objections. 'But no more. By his first wedding anniversary Flynn will be in charge.'

'The company is supposed to come to you,' Ezekiel said.

Zeke shook his head. 'I don't want it. Flynn does. He's your son, as much as I am, and he's earned it a lot more than I have. It's his.'

Ezekiel watched him for a long moment, obviously weighing up how much he wanted This Minute against how much he hated his son right then. Zeke waited. He knew that his father's pride wouldn't allow him to let This Minute go to his main rival. Plus he probably thought he'd be able to get out of stepping down somehow.

He wouldn't. Zeke's lawyers were very, very good at what they did, and they would make sure the contract was watertight. But he'd let the old man hope for now.

'Fine,' Ezekiel said eventually.

Zeke jumped to his feet. 'I'll have my team draw up the papers. They'll be with you by next week.'

'And what about you? What are you going to do?'

Zeke paused in the doorway and smiled at his father. 'I'm going to go and live my own life at last.'

CHAPTER THIRTEEN

ISABELLA WAS WAITING for her in the hallway with the stylist when Thea finally pulled herself together for long enough to make it out of the library. Flynn still hovered nervously at her shoulder, but she tried to give him reassuring smiles when she could, in the hope that he might leave her alone for a few minutes.

'Thea! We're running behind schedule already, you know. And you look dreadful!'

'Thanks,' Thea said, even though she knew her mother-in-law-to-be was probably completely correct.

'Sorry. But…well, you do. Now, come with me and Sheila, here, will get you sorted out. Flynn, I think your father is looking for you. I saw Zeke come out of his office a few moments ago, so God only knows what that is about. Why don't you go and find out?'

Was Isabella just trying to get rid of Flynn for

a moment? Thea wondered. Or did Ezekiel really want him? And, if so, why? Had Zeke finally agreed to sell This Minute to them?

And why did she still care?

It was business, that was all, Thea told herself. It was all business from here on in.

'Will you be okay?' Flynn asked.

'Oh, Flynn, don't be ridiculous. Of course she will! It's her wedding day.'

But Flynn was still looking at Thea, and ignoring his mother, so she nodded. 'I'll be fine. Go.'

Flynn gave her an uncertain smile. 'Okay. I'll see you at the church.'

'At the church,' Thea agreed weakly.

Sheila had set up in Thea's bedroom, so she followed the stylist and Isabella up the stairs, trying to focus on what happened next. One foot in front of the other—that was the way. One small step at a time until she was married and safe. Easy.

'So, what are we doing with your hair, then?' Sheila asked. 'Did you decide? I think all the styles we tried looked good on you, so really it's up to you.'

Thea tried and failed to remember what any of the practice styles had looked like. It had been days ago, before Zeke arrived. And everything before then was rapidly fading into a blur.

'I liked the curls,' Isabella said. 'With the front pinned up and the veil over the ringlets. It looked so dramatic with your dark hair. Don't you think, Thea?'

'Uh, sure. Sounds good.'

'Great!' Sheila said brightly, obviously used to brides almost comatose on their wedding day. Did everyone feel like this? Shell-shocked? Even if they hadn't been through the sort of drama Thea had in the last few days, did every bride have this moment of disbelief? This suspended reality?

Maybe it was just her.

Sheila started fussing with her hair and Thea sat back and let it happen, focussing on the feel of the strands as they were pinned, the warmth of the straighteners as the stylist used them to form ringlets. There was a strange calm in the room as Isabella flicked through a magazine and Sheila got to work, but still Thea had the feeling that she was being watched by her jailer as she was restrained.

Crazy. She'd shake her head to dispel the notion, but Sheila might burn her with the straighteners.

'Thea!'

The door burst open at the same time as Helena's shout came, and Sheila wisely stepped back before Thea spun round.

'What's happened?' Thea asked. Even Isabella closed her magazine for the moment.

'Zeke's leaving!'

Oh. That. 'I know.'

'He's supposed to be the best man!'

'Daniel's going to stand in, I think.'

'Right.' Helena leant back against the door. 'And…you're okay with this?'

'Helena,' Isabella said, putting her magazine aside and getting to her feet. 'Why don't we let your sister finish getting ready? Go and check on the centrepieces and the bouquets. Then you can come and have your hair done next. Okay?'

'Right. Sure.' Helena's brow crinkled as she looked at Thea. 'Unless you need me for…anything?'

Thea gave her a faint smile. 'I'm fine,' she lied. 'You'll come and help me get into my dress later, though, yeah?'

'Of course,' Helena promised as Isabella ushered her out of the door—presumably in case her little sister gave her the chance to reconsider her decision to marry Flynn.

Thea settled back into her chair, feeling comfortably numb and barely noticing that Isabella had left with Helena. It was almost time, and Zeke was almost gone.

There was nothing to reconsider.

Zeke had almost expected the knock at his door. Placing a roughly folded shirt on top of the clothes already in his case, he turned and called, 'Come in.'

His mother looked older, somehow, than she had since his return. Maybe it was just that she'd let the perma-smile drop for a moment.

'You're leaving me again, then?'

'Not just you,' Zeke pointed out, turning back to his wardrobe to retrieve the last of his shirts.

'I don't imagine you were planning on saying goodbye this time, either.'

Isabella moved to sit on the bed, to one side of his suitcase. The one place in the room he couldn't hope to ignore her.

'I wasn't sure you'd miss me any more this time than last,' he said, dropping another shirt into the case. 'What with the wedding to focus on. And I'm sure you have plans for marrying Helena off to someone convenient next.'

Picking up the shirt, Isabella smoothed out the creases as she folded it perfectly. 'I suppose I should be grateful that you're not staying to ruin Thea's wedding.'

Zeke stopped, turned, and stared. 'Thea's wedding? Not Flynn's?' He shook his head. 'You know, for years I never understood why you cared so much more about someone else's children than your own. I guess I thought it must be because they were girls, or because you felt sorry for them after their mother died. I can't believe it took me until now to realise it was because you thought they should have been yours.'

'I don't know what you're talking about,' Isabelle said, her gaze firmly fixed on the shirt. 'I loved all four of you equally. Even Flynn.'

'Ha! *That*, right there, shows me what a lie that is.' Grabbing the shirt from her, he shoved it into the case, making her look up at him. 'Why didn't you just leave, Mum? And marry Thomas? It can't have been for our sakes. We'd have been downright grateful!'

'My place is at my husband's side.' She folded her hands in her lap and met his eyes at last. 'Whatever else, I am his wife first and foremost.'

Zeke stared at her in amazement. 'You're wrong. You're *yourself* first.'

She gave him a sad smile. 'No, Zeke. That's just you.'

Zeke grabbed his case, tugging the zip roughly round it. He'd probably forgotten something, but he could live without it. He had his passport and his wallet. Everything else was replaceable. *Except Thea.*

'Do you even know how you made us feel all those years?' He wasn't coming back again. He could afford to tell her the truth. 'You let our father pit us against each other like it was a sport, and you ran off to another man's family whenever we weren't enough for you. For years I felt like an unwanted accident, every bit as much as Flynn felt like the outsider.'

'That's not…that's not how it was.'

'It's how it felt,' Zeke told her, pressing the truth home. 'And when I left… Thomas says that you missed me. That I broke your heart. But, Mum, how would I even know?'

'Of course I missed you. You're my son.'

'But you never thought to contact me. I wasn't hiding, Mum. I was right there if you needed me.'

'You made your feelings about our family very clear when you left.'

She still sounded so stiff, so unyielding. Zeke shook his head. Maybe her pride would always be too much for her to get over. Maybe his had been too, until now. But he'd already cut all ties with his father—could he really afford to do the same with his mother?

'I'm going now, Mum. And to be honest I'm not going to be coming back in a hurry. Maybe not ever. But if you mean it—about missing me—call me some time.' He lifted his carry-on bag onto his shoulder. 'Goodbye, Mum.'

But she was already looking away.

Outside his room, the corridors were cool and empty. He supposed most people would be in their rooms, getting ready for the wedding. A few were probably already down at the church, making sure they got a good seat for the wedding of the year. If he was quick he could grab one of the taxis milling about and be on his way to the airport before anyone even said 'I do'.

'Dad says that you're leaving.'

Zeke stopped at the top of the stairs at the sound of his brother's voice ahead of him. So close. And now he'd have to deal with all three family members in the space of an hour. At least it was the last time.

'Well, yeah,' he said, turning slowly and leaning his case against the wall. 'Not a lot of reason to stay now.'

'Is that truly the only reason you came back? For Thea?' Flynn asked. 'To try and win her back, I mean.'

'No. I thought…' With a sigh, Zeke jogged down a few steps to meet his brother in the middle of the staircase. 'I thought I'd moved on. From her, from the family, from everything. I came back to prove that to myself, I guess.'

'Did it work?'

Zeke smiled ruefully. 'Not entirely as planned, no. Turns out I was a little more tied in to things here than I thought.'

'And now?'

'Now I'm done,' Zeke said firmly. 'Ask our father.'

'I did.' Hitching his trousers, Flynn sat on the step, right in the middle of the stairs.

After a moment Zeke followed suit. 'I feel about five, sitting on the stairs,' he said.

Flynn laughed. 'We used to—do you remember? When Mum and Dad had parties, when we were really little, we'd sneak out of bed and sit on the stairs, watching and listening.'

'I remember,' Zeke said. He must have been no more than four or five then. Had he known, or sensed, even then that he and Flynn were different? Or rather that their father believed they were?

'Dad told me your terms for selling This Minute to Morrison-Ashton.'

Zeke glanced up at his brother. 'All of them?'

Flynn ticked them off on his fingers. 'No role for you, Director of Digital Media for Thea, and...' Flynn caught Zeke's gaze and held it. 'CEO for me.'

'That's right.' Zeke dipped his head to avoid his brother's eyes.

'It was yours, you know,' Flynn said. 'I always knew that in the end Dad would give it to you. You're Ashton blood, after all.'

'I don't want it,' Zeke said. 'And you deserve it.'

'I'll do a better job at it, too.'

Zeke laughed. 'You will. I want to build things, then move on. You want to make things run smoothly. You're the best choice for it.'

'Was that the only reason?'

Zeke stared out over the hallway of the villa, all decked out in greenery and white flowers, with satin ribbons tied in bows to everything that stayed still long enough for the wedding planner to attack. 'No. I wanted to show Dad that his plan hadn't worked.'

'His plan? You mean, the way he always pitted us against each other?'

'Yeah. I wanted him to know that despite everything, all his best efforts, you were still my brother. Blood or not.'

Flynn stretched his legs out down the stairs and leant back on his elbows. 'You know, that would sound a whole lot more sincere and meaningful if you hadn't slept with my fiancée last night.'

Zeke winced. 'Yeah, I guess so. Look, I'm...' He trailed off. He wasn't sorry—not really. He hadn't done it to hurt his brother, but he couldn't regret having one more night with Thea. 'That wasn't about you. It was about Thea and I saying goodbye to each other.'

'That's not what you wanted it to be, though, is it?'

'Maybe not.' Zeke shrugged. 'But it's the way it is. She wants a different life to the one I'm offering. And I need to live my life away from the bitterness this family brings out in me.'

'She told you that, huh?'

'Yeah.'

'So I guess I have her to thank for my promotion, really?'

'Hey! I played my part, too.'

'Let's just agree to call it quits, then, yeah?'

'Sounds like a plan.' Although Zeke had to think that all Flynn had got out of that deal was a company. He'd got to sleep with Thea. Clearly he was winning.

Except after today Flynn would get to sleep with Thea whenever he wanted. And Zeke would be alone.

Maybe Flynn was winning after all, even if he *did* have to deal with their parents and Morrison-Ashton for the rest of time.

'But, Zeke, after today… She's off-limits, yeah?'

'I know.' Zeke grabbed hold of the banister and pulled himself up. 'It's not going to be a problem. As soon as I'm packed I'll grab a cab to the airport and leave you guys to get on with your happy-ever-after.'

'You're not coming back?' Flynn asked.

Zeke shook his head. 'Not for a good while, at least. I need to…I need to find something else to make my life about, you know?'

'Not really,' Flynn said with a half-smile. 'I've spent my whole life trying to get in to this family, while you've spent it trying to get out.'

'I guess so.' Zeke wondered how it would feel to finally get the one thing you'd always wanted. Maybe he'd never know. 'Something you and Thea have in common.'

Flynn tilted his head as he stared up at him. 'You really love her, don't you?'

Zeke shrugged, and stepped past his brother to climb the stairs to retrieve his suitcase. 'Love doesn't matter now.'

CHAPTER FOURTEEN

'Wow,' Helena said as Thea stepped out from behind the screen. 'Maybe you should just walk down the aisle like that. I'm sure Flynn wouldn't complain. Or any of the male guests.'

Thea pulled a face at her sister in the mirror. She wasn't even sure she looked like herself. From the ringlets and veil, to the excess layers of make-up Sheila had assured her were necessary to 'last through the day'—despite the fact the wedding was at four in the afternoon—she looked like someone else. A bride, she supposed.

She let her gaze drop lower in the mirror, just long enough to take in the white satin basque that pushed her breasts up into realms they'd never seen before and the sheer white stockings that clipped onto the suspenders dangling from the basque. She looked like a stripper bride. She hoped Flynn would appreciate it.

Zeke would have.

Not thinking about that.

'Help me into the dress?' Thea said, turning away from the mirror. 'We're late already, and I think the wedding planner is about to have a heart attack. She's been calling from the church every five minutes to check where we are.'

Helena reached up to take the heavy ivory silk concoction from its hanger, then paused, biting her lip as she looked back at Thea.

'Don't, Helena,' Thea said, forestalling whatever objection her sister was about to raise. 'Just pass me the dress, yeah?'

Helena unhooked the dress and held it up for Thea to step into. Then, as Thea wriggled it over her hips, pulling it up over the basque, Helena said, 'Are you sure about this? I mean, really, *really* sure?'

Thea sighed. 'Trust me, Helena. You are not the only person to ask me that today. But I've made my decision. I'm marrying Flynn.'

'I'm glad to hear it.'

Thea spun around at the words, to see Flynn leaning against the doorframe.

'What are you *doing here*?' The last couple of words came out as a shriek, but Thea didn't care.

'I need to tell you something,' Flynn said, perfectly reasonably. 'It's important.'

'Not *now*!'

'You look beautiful, by the way,' Flynn added, as if that meant anything. The groom wasn't allowed to see the bride in her wedding dress before the wedding! It was terrible, *terrible* luck!

'Flynn, why don't you tell her what you came to tell her so she can stop freaking out?' Helena suggested. 'Plus, you should be down at the church already.'

Flynn nodded his agreement. 'Zeke has agreed to sell This Minute to Morrison-Ashton.'

Thea stopped trying to cover up her dress with her arms and stared at him. 'Seriously? *Why*?'

'Probably because someone convinced him he had to leave everything here behind and find his own path in life.'

'Ah,' Helena said, eyes wide. 'Thea, what—?'

'It doesn't matter.' Thea cut her off. 'Does that mean he's not taking the director job?'

'No. He insisted that Dad give that to you.'

Thea started to shake. Just a tremor in her hands and arms to start with, but she could feel it spreading.

'And he's made Dad agree to step down within the next year and pass the company to me,' Flynn finished. Even he looked a little shell shocked at that bit.

Thea dropped into the nearest chair as the tremors hit her knees. 'Why? Why would he do that?'

But she already knew. He'd given in. He'd given his father exactly what he wanted so he could walk away clear and free. Just as she'd told him he'd never be able to do.

'I think he wanted to make things right,' Flynn said, and Thea felt the first tear hit her cheek.

Zeke was free of them all at last. Even her. And she was being left behind again, still trying to prove she was good enough to belong. After today she'd be tied in for ever, never able to walk away.

Was she *jealous*?

'Thea? Are you okay?' Helena asked.

'No!' Thea sobbed, the word a violent burst of sound. 'I'm a mess. I'm a mistake.'

'That's not true,' Helena said soothingly, and Thea could see her giving Flynn looks of wide-eyed concern. 'What would make you think that?'

Thea gave a watery chuckle. 'Oh, I don't know. Maybe sleeping with the best man the night before my wedding? Perhaps having to have an intervention with my almost-mother-in-law about how it was better to have an affair than marry an inappropriate guy?'

Flynn swore at that, Thea was pleased to note.

'Or maybe sending away the guy I love so I can marry the guy I'm supposed to? And now, on top of everything else, Flynn's seen me in my wedding dress. That's not just like pearls! Everyone knows that's *absolute* bad luck! It's against all the rules!'

With another glance back at Flynn—who, Thea was frustrated to note, was still standing perfectly calmly in the doorway, with just a slight look of discomfort on his face—Helena knelt down beside her.

'Thea. I don't think this is about rules any more.'

'No. It's about me messing up again. I was so close to being happy here! And now I'm making a mess of everything.'

Helena shook her head. 'No, you're not. And today's not about family, or business, or any of the other things you seem to think this wedding should be about.'

Thea looked up at her sister. 'Then what *is* it about?'

'It's about love,' Helena said. 'It's about trusting your heart to know the right thing to do. And, since you're sitting here sobbing in a designer wedding dress, I think your heart is trying to tell you something.'

It couldn't, Thea wanted to say, because it had stopped. Her heart had stopped still in her chest the moment Zeke had walked out of the library that morning, so it couldn't tell her anything.

But her head could. And it was screaming at her right now that she was an idiot. She'd spent so long trying to find her place in the world, trying to force her way into a role that had never been right for her, she'd ignored the one place she truly belonged all along.

She looked up at Flynn, still so calm and serene and perfect—but not perfect for her.

'Go,' he said, a faint smile playing on his lips. 'You might still catch him.'

'But…but what about the wedding? Everyone's here, and our parents are waiting, and—'

'We'll take care of it,' Helena promised, glancing over at Flynn.

Was there something in that look? Had Isabella been right? Thea couldn't be sure.

'Won't we?'

'We will,' Flynn agreed. 'All you have to do now is run.'

Somewhere in the villa a door slammed, and Thea knew it had to be Zeke, leaving her again. But this time she was going with him.

Shoving the heavy wedding dress back down over her hips, Thea stepped out of it and dashed for the door, pausing only for a second to kiss Flynn lightly on the cheek. 'Thanks,' she said.

And then she ran.

Zeke shut the front door to the villa behind him and walked out into the late-afternoon Tuscan sun. Everyone must have already headed down to the little chapel at the bottom of the hill, ready for the wedding. His talk with Flynn had delayed him, and now there were no taxis hanging around. He might be able to find one down at the church, but he didn't want to get that close to the main event. Not with Thea due to make her grand entrance any time now. The wedding planner's schedule had her down there already, he remembered, unless they were running late.

No, he'd call for a cab and sit out here in the sunshine while he waited. One last glimpse of his old life before he started his new one.

Phone call made, he settled onto the terrace, sitting on the edge of the warm stone steps rather than the swing seat round at the side. Too many memories. Besides, he wouldn't see the cab arrive.

He heard a car in the distance and stood, hefting his carry-on bag onto his shoulder and tugging up the pull-along handle of his case. No car appeared, though, and he started to think it must have been another guest heading for the chapel. But he made his way down the driveway anyway, just in case.

'Zeke!'

Behind him the door to the villa flew open, and by the time he could turn Thea was halfway down the stairs and racing down the drive towards him.

He blinked in disbelief as she got closer, sunlight glowing behind her, making the white of her outfit shine.

White. But not her wedding dress.

'Isn't this where I came in?' he asked, waving

a hand towards her to indicate the rather skimpy lingerie that was doing wonderful things for her heaving cleavage as she tried to get her breath back.

'Don't,' she said, scowling.

'Don't what?' Zeke asked. 'You're the one chasing me in your underwear. Five more minutes and my cab would have been here and I'd have been out of your life, just as you wanted.'

'Don't joke. Don't mock. I need you to…' She took a deep breath. 'I need you to stop being… you know…*you* for a moment. Because I need to tell you something.'

'What?' Zeke dropped his bag to the ground again. Apparently this was going to take a while.

'I don't want you out of my life.'

Zeke's breath caught in his chest—until he realised what she was *actually* saying. 'Thea, I can't. I can't just stick around and be Uncle Zeke for Christmas and birthdays. You were right; I need a fresh start. A clean break. Besides…' *I can't watch you live happily ever after with my brother when I'm totally in love with you myself.*

But Thea was shaking her head. 'That's not what I mean.'

'Then *what*, Thea?' Zeke asked, exasperated. He'd so nearly been done. So nearly broken free for good. And here he was, having this ridiculous conversation with Thea in her underwear, when she was supposed to be getting married *right now.*

Unless…

'I've spent all day listening to people tell me what I should do. What's best for me. Where my place is. And I'm done. You were right—but don't let it go to your head. I need to make my own decisions. So I'm making one right now. I'm choosing my home, my place in the world. And it's the only choice that's going to matter ever again.'

She stepped closer, and Zeke's hands itched to take hold of her, to pull her close. But this was her decision, and she had to make it all on her own. And he had to let her.

'I'm choosing you,' she whispered, so close that he could feel the words against his lips. 'For better or worse, for mistake or for happily-ever-after, for ever and ever.'

Zeke stared into her soft blue eyes and saw no doubt hiding there. No uncertainty, no fear. She meant this.

'You're sure,' he said, but it wasn't a question. He knew.

'I'm certain. I love you. More than anything.'

Thea's hands wrapped around him to run up his back, and the feel of her through his shirt made him warmer.

'I should have known it sooner. *You're* my place. *You're* where I belong.'

'I can't stay here, Thea,' he said. 'Maybe we can come back, but I need some time away. I'm done obsessing about the past. It's time to start my own life.'

'I know.' Thea smiled. 'I'm the one who told you that, remember?'

'I remember.' Unable to resist any longer, Zeke dipped his head and kissed her, long and sweet and perfect. 'I love you. I thought when I came back that I was looking for the girl I'd known— the one I loved as a boy. But I couldn't have imagined the woman you'd become, Thea. Or how much more I'd love you now.'

Thea buried her laugh in his chest. 'I'm the same. I thought it would kill me, saying goodbye to you last time. But the thought of living the rest of my life without you…' She shook her head and reached up to kiss him again.

'Unacceptable.' Zeke finished the thought for her. And then he asked the question that had echoed through his mind for eight long years, hoping he'd get a different answer this time. 'Will you come with me?'

Thea smiled up at him and said, 'Always.'

And Zeke knew, at last, that it didn't matter where they went, or who led and who followed. They'd always be together, and that was all he needed.

* * * * *

If you enjoyed Thea and Zeke's story look out for Helena and Flynn's, early in 2015!

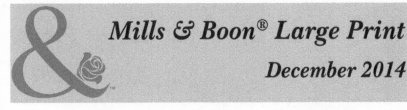

Mills & Boon® Large Print

December 2014

Mills & Boon® Large Print
January 2015

THE HOUSEKEEPER'S AWAKENING
Sharon Kendrick

MORE PRECIOUS THAN A CROWN
Carol Marinelli

CAPTURED BY THE SHEIKH
Kate Hewitt

A NIGHT IN THE PRINCE'S BED
Chantelle Shaw

DAMASO CLAIMS HIS HEIR
Annie West

CHANGING CONSTANTINOU'S GAME
Jennifer Hayward

THE ULTIMATE REVENGE
Victoria Parker

INTERVIEW WITH A TYCOON
Cara Colter

HER BOSS BY ARRANGEMENT
Teresa Carpenter

IN HER RIVAL'S ARMS
Alison Roberts

FROZEN HEART, MELTING KISS
Ellie Darkins

1214 Rom LP

MILLS & BOON®

Why shop at millsandboon.co.uk?

Each year, thousands of romance readers find their perfect read at millsandboon.co.uk. That's because we're passionate about bringing you the very best romantic fiction. Here are some of the advantages of shopping at www.millsandboon.co.uk:

* **Get new books first**—you'll be able to buy your favourite books one month before they hit the shops

* **Get exclusive discounts**—you'll also be able to buy our specially created monthly collections, with up to 50% off the RRP

* **Find your favourite authors**—latest news, interviews and new releases for all your favourite authors and series on our website, plus ideas for what to try next

* **Join in**—once you've bought your favourite books, don't forget to register with us to rate, review and join in the discussions

Visit **www.millsandboon.co.uk**
for all this and more today!

MILLS_WEB_LP